FATE OF THE DEMON

Witch of the Lake Book Two

MIRANDA HONFLEUR
NICOLETTE ANDREWS

Cover art by KD Ritchie at Storywrappers

Map by Rela "Kellerica" Similä

Proofreading by Anthony S. Holabird and Lea Vickery

Paperback ISBN: 978-1-949932-16-4

Enclave Boxed Sets

Of Beasts and Beauties

WORLD OF AKATSUKI

Tales of Akatsuki Series

Kitsune: A Little Mermaid Retelling

Yuki: A Snow White Retelling

Okami: A Little Red Riding Hood Retelling

Dragon Saga

The Priestess and the Dragon (Book 1)

The Sea Stone (Book 2)

The Song of the Wind (Book 3)

The Fractured Soul (Book 4)

DIVINER'S WORLD

Duchess

"Sorcerer" (available at
www.fantasyauthornicoletteandrews.com)

Diviner's Prophecy

Diviner's Curse

Diviner's Fate

Princess

This book is for...

J.M. Butler, Katherine Bennet, Anthony Holabird, Lea Vickery, Alisha Klapheke, Alistair North, Andrea Peel, Ashley Martinez, Barbara Harrison, Charity Chimni, Charley Curry, Chloe Bratt-Lewis, Clare Sager, Cyndy Shubert-Jett, Dana S. Jackson Lange, Darlene Kunst Rooney, Deb Barringer, Deborah Dunson, Donna Adamek, Donna Levett, Donna Swenson, Emily Allen West, Emily Wiebe, Erin McDonough, Erin Miller, Eugenia Kollia, Fanny Comas, Fiona Andrew, Jackie Tansky, Janel Iverson, Jennifer Hoblitt Kaser, Jennifer Moriarity, Jennifer Robertson, Judith Cohen, Karen Borges, Kathy Brown, Kelly Scott, Kimberly, Kris Walls, Kristen White, Krys Baxter-Ragsdale, Linda Adams, Linda Levine, Linda Romer, Lyn Andreasen, Maggie Borges, Marilyn Smith, Marla Ramsey, Mary Nguyen, Michelle Ferreira, Nicole Page, Patrycja Pakula, Rachel Cass, Roger Fauble, Samantha Mikals, Scarolet Ellis, Seraphia Sparks, Shannon Childress, Shauna Joesten, Shelby Palmer, Shivani Kitson, Spring Runyon, Susanne Huxhorn, Tanya Wheeler, Teri Ruscak, Tina Carter, Tony Sommer, Tricia Wright, Vicki Michelle, Wanda Wozniczka...

...and everyone else who's supported us and spread the word about our books from the start. We couldn't do this without you, and you being in our corner has meant the world to us.

FATE OF THE DEMON

To Tony and Drew,
whom we chose once and, in an instant,
would choose again.

The Village Of
CZARNOBRZEG

Listen. .
   With faint dry sound,
   Like steps of passing ghosts,
   The leaves, frost-crisp'd, break from the trees
   And fall.

— ADELAIDE CRAPSEY, "NOVEMBER
NIGHT" (1922)

CHAPTER 1

The twisted horns weighed down Brygida's head as she drew the cottage door shut, careful not to make a sound. With the size as great as a stag's antlers, there was no avoiding a little heaviness, but she'd hollowed out the twigs she'd used. The *lejiń* demon's costume would appease Weles tonight, or so she hoped.

In the night's cloak, her breath bloomed in the wintry air. She tugged her voluminous bear fur closer, securing it with a clawed belt over her good dress. As the year turned further toward its end, the cold greedily devoured more and more of each day. And tonight, there was no more left of warmth but a gnawed bone, chilled to the marrow.

The dark winter woods rested in silence tonight, even its apparitions haunting the withered undergrowth in eerie quiet. The reverent oaks had shed their crowns of leaves, bowing bare limbs to Weles.

A swift crack echoed in the clear air, followed by a thud—Mama splitting firewood in the garden, evidently with the duller axe. This wasn't for their hearth, then, but for Mama's own inner fire. On days when Mama's frustrations ate away at her patience, she often took to the garden and the duller axe like fire to tinder. It was a habit of Mama's she had inherited, at least in some way, because when her own frustrations hungered, there wasn't a single bit of the cottage that didn't get scrubbed. Days of fighting at home often spoke in heaping wood piles and gleaming surfaces.

She crept to the edge of the cottage and waited like a mouse under a broom, biding her time until the coast was clear.

"Come inside, Ewa," Mamusia's light voice entreated.

A brusque huff answered. "She's not going, and that's the end of it," Mama grumbled. "The peace has been precarious, and she's not thinking about the future—"

A soft sigh. "She's thinking about tonight."

Leaning against the ash-wood beams, Brygida bit her lip. Tonight...

Tonight she'd be entering a new world, one she was utterly unprepared for. Like falling into a winter stream, it made her shiver, but the unknown always did. It was the world that kind, thoughtful Kaspian inhabited, and that was all she needed to know. Like the seed anticipating the coming spring, she would put her trust in him and step forward. He'd protect her from his familiar dangers, and against all the rest, she would protect them both.

"You know it only takes one woman," Mama murmured between resounding strikes of the axe.

One woman. Yes, the Mrok witches' wrath of the blood came from Holy Mokosza, and that meant it couldn't be used to harm women. A peasant woman could hurt her, possibly, but no one in the village wanted that, least of all the women. It was for their protection that Holy Mokosza had cultivated the Mrok bloodline here.

"This one night may bring grave consequences," Mama finished grimly.

"And its forbidding may bring a lifetime of regret." Mamusia's words of caution left a lengthy silence breathing in their wake. "Let the children have this."

For so long, Mamusia had sheltered her just as forbiddingly as Mama had, and it hadn't been without reason. In a haze of prophecy, Mamusia had dreamed her end—death at the hands of a man—but when Julian's grip had tightened around her throat, had that prophetic dream been sated? Mamusia had seemed to think so, and she even argued as though the danger had passed. Her prophecies, after all, were always certain and yet never clear. But this interpretation seemed the likeliest.

A tiny bud of hope blossomed in her chest. Mamusia was on her side, so Mama would be sure to follow. Holy Mokosza would topple her loom the day Mama would refuse her anything for long.

At long last, an exasperated grunt—Mama's. Footsteps crunched, breaking the snow briskly, louder and louder.

Pressed tight against the wall, Brygida didn't move, didn't breathe. Maybe Mama wouldn't notice her, and she could avoid yet another lecture—

Flowing blond locks breezed past her as Mamusia passed by and twirled, a little smile curling her lips and her violet eyes sparkling in the moonlight. A pleased sparkle, if looks did not deceive?

Brygida raised her mask, careful not to hit the cottage with the horns. Her mouth dropped open, but no words came out. It was a singular day that saw Mamusia championing an excursion beyond their witchlands, but here they were.

Mamusia leaned in and gave her a once-over. "Bear fur?" she whispered.

Stifling a laugh, Brygida shrugged a shoulder. It wouldn't have been her first choice for appearance's sake, but bear fur had a certain kind of magic, and when it came to appeasing Weles, she would take all the magic she could get. "For success, and wisdom."

Mamusia gave her a sage nod, her left eye squinted playfully. "There's a legend that bears are cursed humans trapped inside animals, you know."

With a toothy grin, Brygida tugged the bear-fur cloak open. No human trapped inside a beast tonight.

Mamusia covered her mouth and muffled that easy giggle. "Good. Go, with my blessing and beneath Holy Mokosza's watchful gaze." But for a moment, Mamusia's mirth faded. "But Brygida... I... For nearly your entire life, I have argued to keep you isolated, all because I misinterpreted a prophecy. But I dreamed of red eyes in the woods." Her gaze meandered to a dark thicket, where the unknown lurked in the shadows. "It could be symbolic of unrest, just a sign, you see? Even so... stay on your guard." With a sober nod, she leaned in closer. "And remember to have fun."

Brygida half-laughed under her breath. There was danger, always, but they couldn't spend their lives constantly looking over their shoulders. They had to trust themselves, and each other, to prevail by the grace of Holy Mokosza's divine-given strength. Mamusia acknowledged that now. If only Mama could be so reasonable.

After all, Julian had been rightfully judged; Kaspian had been proven innocent. The village women still sought out their cottage for healing, midwifery, remedies, and last rites. But for a few malcontents, Czarnobrzeg seemed a bloom unfurled for the bees.

And tonight would be splendid with celebration. And Kaspian.

Mamusia patted her shoulder, and with that, she departed for the front door with a light step and a sure-footed gait. Had she ever attended a village celebration? It had never come up, but doubtless the people would've loved her, with her easy smile, gentle way, and earnest good cheer. Not to mention, there were deer not nearly as graceful as Mamusia, and tonight, with all the dancing, was it too much to hope that her grace would be hereditary? Brygida took a deep, bracing breath.

Her entire life, she'd known only the simple pleasures of the forest, the blessings and rites of the Mrok blood, and the company of fairies, animals, trees, demons, and ghosts. Nothing so grand as luxurious feasts, dances in castle halls, and village songs to the tune of exotic instruments. Her meals before the fire, humble rituals, and primeval chants were small by comparison, and... so was she. There was the possibility that the villagers would see her as unworthy, unwelcome, un...civilized.

But they all celebrated the winter solstice, the same festival of Kolęda honoring Weles, didn't they? The spirit of Kolęda lay in sharing, fortune-telling, unity, the spirit underlying the earth's revival. And hospitality, tonight most especially, was a divine duty. Anything less than the utmost reverence that would curse the upcoming year's harvest and risk the ire of Weles, and no one would risk that. No one.

And the dream of red eyes in the wood, well, was only symbolic of some remaining unrest. Nothing more.

Tonight would go well. It would.

With a nod to herself, Brygida put her mask back in place, took a bold step forward, and headed for the castle in Czarnobrzeg.

And for Kaspian.

CHAPTER 2

Today was going to be perfect. It had to be.

Kaspian paced the length of the hall, chin cradled between thumb and forefinger. Servants flitted in and out of the kitchen doorway. Pots and pans clanged, drowning out the sharp commands of Cook as she directed the kitchen help. The intoxicating scent of roasting mackerel perfumed the air and clung to the clothes of bustling servants, making last-minute adjustments to linens and place settings. He shadowed them as they examined platters and cups for stray water spots, casting a critical eye on the alignment of forks and knives.

Everything had to go smoothly. Mere weeks had passed since his name had been cleared and he'd won the support of his people. It still felt tenuous. His older brother Henryk's misdeeds—and the lengths to which

Mama and Tata had gone to hide them—had been revealed. After all of it, the Wolski family owed far more to the people than could ever be repaid. But he would make it his life's mission to do everything in his power for the village's sake. Beginning with a bounteous feast, they could all reforge the kinship that had broken with Roksana's murder and Julian's evil.

The Kolęda festival was one of the rare occasions when the peasants and nobility mingled. In years past, it had been nothing but another of many formal obligations, but this year it was different. And it was also Brygida's first.

Well, her first with the village. As they'd strolled through the winter woods, she'd told him of her family's Kolęda traditions, rites under the moon, incantations and offerings made to Weles. Tonight, Brygida would be entering his world. It paled in comparison to the awe and majesty of the forest, but he just hoped it would live up to her expectations.

The corners of his mouth turned up, and he couldn't help it; at the thought of her, they always did. For him, after years and years of observing the same traditions, the wonder of them had faded some. But the light in her eyes when she experienced something new, it cast a new glow on that faded wonder, awakening depths that had hidden even from himself. He wanted to show her Czarnobrzeg's celebration of Kolęda, and he wanted to show her everything. Every single thing new or unknown to her, just to watch that light in her eyes again and again, as many times as he possibly could in this life, and by her side hope to feel even the barest glow of warmth to awaken those hidden depths of his own.

Outside, the frigid wind howled, like the lamenting cry of a wolf. It rattled shutters, trying to creep in through the cracks in the walls and roof.

Servants worked hard to keep the hall heated; hunched over by the fireplace, one prodded embers to life, and another worked the bellows, while a third fed fresh logs to the flames. Shadows danced over the stone hearth's facade, and golden light illuminated the hall, catching on the silverware, sparkling like stars.

A single trickle of sweat rolled down his shoulder blades as he stopped, his back to the hearth, and eyed the table's place settings. Four. Tata, Stryjek, Mama, and him.

No place for Brygida?

She was—

She... She wasn't a noble, but she wasn't a peasant either. To him, she...

Taking a drawn-out breath, he glared at the empty space beside his own. Clearly, Mama had tried to make a statement with this, and now she'd left him no choice but to meddle with seating arrangements, and plates and chairs and all the other minutiae he'd never given a passing thought to.

With a grunt, he strode toward the table—and collided with a serving woman carrying a stack of plates. It fell to the ground with a thunderous crash.

All heads in the hall swiveled toward the noise. Perun's bright lightning, could nothing go according to plan today?

"My apologies, my lord." The servant scrambled to gather up the plates. No doubt the household was no happier than he was about his interloping.

"Let me." Kaspian bent down to help. "I should have been paying more attention," he said, holding out the last plate. "If it's not too much trouble, there's a place setting missing at the head table. Could you set it for me?"

"Right away, my lord." She bobbed her head before she carried her stack over to the head table.

"What are you doing wasting time, worrying about place settings?" A firm hand clapped him on the back. Stryjek Andrzej, his uncle, grinned at him.

Kaspian rubbed the nape of his neck. "I should be worried. This is the one night we open our doors to the peasantry, and I will be their lord after all, so I want to keep them happy." After everything that had happened recently, he wanted to keep the people happy, both as their future lord and for Brygida's sake. Tonight was the first step to bridging the gap between their worlds.

"Life is too short to fret over peasants," Stryjek said

as he picked at his nails, which were stained black from ink.

When Stryjek had shown up just after the first frost, Kaspian had hardly recognized him. Age had carved lines around his smiling mouth, and his once-blond hair had turned snowy white in the past eight years he'd been wandering the countryside.

As a scholar and poet, Stryjek traveled across the regions of Nizina, telling stories and doing the odd scholar's work to earn his keep. And for the first time in Kaspian's memory, he was joining them for Kolęda.

Perhaps if Stryjek had come at any other time, his visit could have been a happy one. Kaspian had fond memories of Stryjek's stories and mischievous antics from when he was a boy. Now all he felt toward him was envy and the life that could have been his. But of course he could never say so. Just another limitation among many.

"You're right. If you'll excuse me, I have some preparations to oversee," Kaspian said with a forced smile, and strode away, hands balled into fists.

Stryjek made it sound simple, but he'd never felt the burden of this responsibility, and he never would. Being born a second son, and third in line to inherit the lordship, Stryjek had done as he'd pleased, lived the life Kaspian had dreamed of before Henryk's vile act had trapped him in this role.

And because of that fact, he had to do better, to make recompense for the sins of his family.

He grasped at his collar, stretching it to let a breath in. This coat, emerald green and made of a fine tiretaine wool, was too small, but finding something that wouldn't make Brygida feel underdressed but also avoid upsetting his parents was a tall task. This would have to do; Brygida's comfort meant more than his own. Considering the villagers still felt uneasy around her, she didn't need any more distress, and this at least was something he could control. Outside of her duties to Mokosza, they were unused to seeing a witch among them. But he planned to change that.

Before he indulged the impulse to go and change— again—he stalked the perimeter of the hall to the head table and confirmed that the extra place had been set. Brygida would sit by his side, a symbol of his endorse- ment of the witches, and an opportunity for the people to grow accustomed to her presence. Even if the servants were opposed, or even the entire village, he would make sure this night would be a memorable one for her.

Besides, everything would be fine. This was Brygida after all, a woman who could drain the blood from a man with a touch and a thought—he shuddered thinking of it. Given her exceptional capabilities, she could certainly handle a few surly villagers, especially together with him.

A decanter of wine had been set out, along with a goblet. He filled it to the brim before taking a large swig. There was nothing for her to fear in his home. And even if the peasants whispered behind her back, he wouldn't allow their wagging tongues to affect her. Tonight would go exactly as planned. They would dance as they should've during the Feast of the Mother...

The night Roksana had been murdered.

He drained the goblet and set it down to refill it again.

"You're drinking already? The guests haven't even arrived," Mama scolded. Her blond hair, now heavily streaked with white, was coiffed on top of her head in a myriad of looping braids bound with crimson linen ribbons, which she always wore at this time of year. She surveyed the busy hall like a queen overlooking her court.

His gut twisted, and he set the goblet back down with a thump. It was time to play the game he and his parents had been at for weeks, in which they acted as though they'd never thought him a rapist and a murderer, and he painted on a forced smile.

"Is there something I can help you with?" He kept his gaze on Iskra, Mama's dog, hovering at her hip. The deep chocolate-brown eyes of his mother's faithful companion held no judgment, no secrets. Unlike her master.

"I'm glad you asked. Lord Granat has just arrived. He'll sit beside you tonight, so keep him company. You should start making connections now..."

Kaspian's head jerked up. "What is he doing here?"

He cleared his throat and pulled at his too-tight collar. It had been weeks since he'd looked Mama in the eye. She'd hidden the truth about Henryk. She'd believed him capable of raping and murdering Roksana. Although he wanted to mend their broken relationship, the wounds felt too raw to even attempt it.

Memories of the Kolęda feasts of his youth crystallized in his chest, jagged shards that only cut. When he'd been little, Mama used to sneak him candies even though he'd already eaten enough to make him sick. Then the entire village would gather before the bonfire to dance all night. Her face would be ruddy from the exertion of overseeing the festivities, and yet she'd continued smiling and laughing, giving in to his childish demands to keep dancing.

But the halcyon days of his youth were gone, leaving behind only shattered remains that reflected how easily she'd lied to him, how easily she'd presumed him capable of utter depravity.

"Lord Granat was passing through on his way to Bursztyn and decided to join us for the feast."

He now knew better than to trust those kind eyes. She was a charming manipulator, and he wouldn't keep falling for her lies. Even with her husband's quickly declining health and strained family bonds, all she could think about was politics.

For as long as he could remember, Lord Granat had been a looming threat over Rubin, wanting it for his own. Once he'd arranged the marriage of his son and heir to the daughter of Lord Bursztyn, it was apparent he would use that consolidated power to consume the much smaller Rubin.

Wolves surrounded their region, ready to devour them alive, and Mama had been integral in keeping them appeased. Lord Granat wouldn't have traveled in the dead of winter without good reason. Was he coming to make threats? Had spies revealed how sick Tata was?

There was something Mama wasn't telling him. Something more. Before, he would have pressed her and gladly offered his assistance. But once Tata died, all of this would fall on his shoulders.

Couldn't he have one night to pretend that Tata's death didn't cast a pall over him, that he wouldn't soon have to grieve that loss, all the while taking on power he wasn't prepared for?

Another servant approached with an extra place setting. Her gaze flickered to the plate Kaspian had set. "My lady, where should I put this?"

"We seem to have too many places set." Mama laughed high and false.

The hall had been crammed with oaken tables and benches. At the head, the most honored guests and family sat, facing outward. He wouldn't leave Brygida to sit amongst the crowd—she was his savior, Roksana's avenger, and she deserved a place of honor.

Kaspian took the plate from the servant and set it on the far end of the bench. "Lord Granat can sit beside you." He met his mother's gaze, where thunderbolts flashed in her livid eyes.

The servant glanced to Mama.

She lowered her chin with a slight shake of her head. The servant backed away, leaving them alone once more.

"I'm only trying to do what's best for you," Mama said quietly.

He wouldn't abandon Brygida to the wolves of the manor just so Mama could move *him*, not so long ago her presumed rapist-murderer son, like a pawn around the dinner table. It was clear she wanted to keep him occupied, and away from what she deemed unsuitable company.

"I can't entertain Lord Granat. I have other plans." He snatched up his goblet and took a step before Mama grasped him by the elbow.

"Kaspian," she breathed, her eyes wide. Did it really come as a shock that after she'd believed him a villain, he wasn't so keen to obey?

"Don't fear, Mama. I'll try my best not to murder anyone," he added icily.

Her face froze. "You are the future Lord of Rubin."

Repeating it didn't change the fact that when he'd been falsely accused and a mob had raised torches and pitchforks against him, thirsted for his blood, even his own mother hadn't believed in him.

He pulled his arm away from her, none too gently. "That's right—*future* lord. Tonight, I am my own man."

CHAPTER 3

In the stillness and the silence, it was almost as if
Brygida were the only one around for miles. Vast,
snowy windswept fields stretched ahead, an
expanse of unbroken white that abutted barely visible
farm houses, their roofs overburdened beneath shrouds
of snow.

As the fleeting days gave way to lengthier nights, the
cold and the dark claiming the land seeped into the
hearts of men; they hid behind walls and fireplaces,
beneath roofs and blankets, waiting for the winter to
break.

Nature, too, waited beneath the cold and the dark,
eager for rebirth, for the turn of the Wheel, and the
anticipation burned in her own blood. Tonight, the
gloom would drown all, black waters over flood lands,

the longest dark of Kolęda lit by that burning hope for light, for warmth, for spring.

She smoothed her hands over the ample bear fur, the bristly guard hairs coarse, and the lingering musk of bear far from comforting, but somehow she felt less alone. The spark of Kolęda hope flared just as brightly in a Mrok witch's heart as in any other, perhaps even more so—or was it only her kind who yearned for this evening as the light, the warmth, and the spring did?

The winter wind blew past, out toward the distance where the glow of a bonfire blazed in the night, haloed by small, winking lights in the grim. Candles—lots of them, tiny flames trying to illuminate the darkest time of the year, help the gods turn the Wheel from winter to spring, and invite the spirits of deceased loved ones to visit. Even in the dark, the way to Czarnobrzeg glittered.

Lively music filtered in, the gęśla and a band of singers, and the winking lights were dancers casting moving silhouettes that swayed with the flames. Merry voices carried from afar. A crowd of people approached from the direction of the village, a procession of masked carolers singing together, and they joined the festivities surrounding the manor house.

Most of them had donned what seemed to be goat costumes, familiar in their animalistic traits and the horns especially, but... far tamer than her demonic *lejiń* attire. Perhaps the villagers believed the threat of a goat herd was enough to scare away demons? At home, she,

Mama, and Mamusia would have all been wearing their most frightening garb, trying their hardest to appease Weles and chase away the winter.

But here, it was far more of a celebration, the like only a multitude of people could provide, and something she'd never experienced on her witchlands. The Feast of the Mother a few weeks ago had come close, but its joy had quickly burned to ash with the violent events of that night.

She fell into step behind the crowd, without so much as a glance back from anyone. Laughter cut the air, loud and carefree, from near the bonfire, its smoky perfume welcome and familiar. A large man, his black hair streaked with gray, raised a cup to his mouth, its beverage running in rivulets down the sides of his face, and then slid a sleeve across his lips. His many rings glinting in the firelight, he clasped arms with a well-dressed man.

Dariusz, Nina's father, with a stranger wealthy enough to afford fine woolen cloth.

It wasn't so long ago that she'd suspected Dariusz of murdering Roksana. His wife, Zofia, had borne the bruises to have made it plausible, but in the end, Julian had proven his own guilt, and his villainy.

With a shudder, she looked over the crowds. She was here as a guest for the Kolęda festivities, but a part of her—the part that had been Mokosza's Reaper of Death only a few weeks ago—took a second look at the men who watched women, attempted to divine their intentions. Julian had been a presence in Roksana's life since her childhood, had been kind to her, had presented himself as a friend and an ally, and yet lurking beneath that congenial mask had been a monster. And here, many men wore congenial masks they had crafted, some by hand and others perhaps by devious intention.

"Mothers, hide your children," a sardonic voice called out, and holding her mask's headdress, she followed the sound. "Men, hold your ladies close. I say, there's a demon among us."

Stefan's dark eyes gleamed in the warm light of the bonfire, matched to a wry smile. Finally, a friendly face.

"Grr," she replied, mustering her best demonic growl.

He canted his head, hands on his hips, and pressed his mouth shut, although the edges twitched. No mask or costume, but he wore a gray robe sashed at the waist with red, longer than his usual tunics and more festive with the added splash of color. He'd slicked back his dark hair, and it reflected the fires like a wolf's eye. "Come now, is that your best growl?"

The smile fled his face and his eyes widened, focused behind her. He reached up a hand.

Her mask brushed up against her face, abruptly pulled off. She squeezed her eyes shut but whirled.

"There *is* a demon among us," Dariusz spat, his face twisted in a hateful sneer.

She swiped for her mask, but he simply raised it higher.

"You're not welcome here." He leaned in, holding her gaze. Firelight flashed red in his eyes.

Stefan stepped between them and, taller, snatched her mask away from him. "Brygida is here by our future lord's personal invitation," he said, his voice low and his face a breath away from Dariusz's smirk. "Isn't there a bottle missing you somewhere? Find your way back to it."

An amused huff, and Dariusz thumbed his jaw casually. "Take care that your stallion doesn't steal onto my fields tonight."

"My stallion finds your fields inviting," he replied with a dark, biting edge. "Perhaps they long for more than an old, clumsy jackass."

Fire stirred in Dariusz's gaze, and it didn't seem to be animals and fields they were discussing.

"Come, come!" an older man's voice beckoned. He wore a long, black hooded robe with the mark of the horned serpent, and held a staff decorated with ever-green sprigs, charred at its base. A special guest representing Weles?

Dariusz and Stefan's locked gazes remained unbroken, but the old man removed Dariusz's arm and then tapped Stefan's shoulder until they turned to him. He pointed toward the bonfire.

"Let us see the future of Rubin together!" the old man beckoned, so merry and mischievous it was difficult not to smile.

The last thing she wanted was for Stefan to come to blows with Dariusz on her account, especially during Kolęda. She hooked her arm in Stefan's, and his gaze flickered to her, its animosity fading. "Stefan, I want to hear all about this 'seeing the future.' Tell me."

Without waiting for his reply, she took her mask from him, put it on, and led them toward the bonfire. The crowd—even Dariusz—gathered around the old man, who lured in every last caroler, his black billowing sleeves raven's wings against the tower of flame. "Come, come, gather around the bonfire and let Weles tell you what the future holds," he bade, his thick voice carrying like a tendril of smoke. "What will come after the snow?"

"Longer days!" someone offered.

"Plentiful crops!" called another.

"Yes, yes," the old man said, drawling theatrically. "The sparks will tell all."

How would the sparks divine the future? She'd never seen such a custom, and now found herself standing straighter, peeking over and between the heads of villagers.

"Willow sparks," Stefan whispered, leaning in

toward her ear. "If they burn long and bright, it'll be a merry fire."

And a merry fire would bode well for the future, with enduring sparks for all to see.

At home, Mama served the good tea and Mamusia would read the leaves. Maybe that was what they were doing now. She shifted from foot to foot, and Stefan rested his hand on her arm, only for a moment. She took a deep, calming breath.

The old man grasped his willow-wrapped staff and approached the fire, where the large logs at its foundation burned molten. He plunged the charred base of the staff into the fire, striking the log at the bottom.

Once, twice, multiple times, and everyone's hands came together to clap to the staff's thudding strikes. Sparks plumed from the glowing wood, myriad fireflies taking flight on the wintry air, soaring into darkness.

And then the thudding stopped.

In the quiet crackling of the bonfire, not a word was spoken nor sung as the crowd held a collective breath, gazes locked on the fiery sparks against the night. Around the bonfire, men carrying torches stepped forward and dipped the ends into the flames. They stepped back together, illuminating the faces of the crowd. The villagers wearing goat masks covered their faces, retreating from the light.

"You're supposed to fear the light, demon," Stefan teased.

And so it was with her family, too. At the lighting of the solar beacons, they would always retreat and remove their masks before returning to the fire as humans.

She nodded and played along, joining the fleeing goat-demons to the fringes of the gathered villagers. Everyone here knew their part without being told. It all came so naturally to them.

The torch-bearers weaved through the crowd, illuminating dormant stacks of firewood with carved sun-discs at their pinnacles. The towers of flame burned bright and high, and other villagers lit their own torches with its flames. As each one caught fire, the night's darkness gave way to their combined dawn-bright glow.

One by one, the villagers removed their masks, until no demons remained, only human faces. She pulled off her own as well, but among the woolen coats and unfamiliar faces, she retreated deeper into her bear fur, keeping to the fringes of the celebration. If Mamusia had interpreted her dream accurately, then perhaps Dariusz wasn't the only malcontented presence here. She wouldn't step into the light unless she had to.

Stefan took up a torch as well, shining the light upon her face, and she squinted against its brightness. It seemed he wouldn't let her hide.

"Now we go inside and feast." He grinned and gestured toward the crowd filing into the manor house.

"But—"

His grin widening, he shook his head. "But nothing. Even out in the woods, you know that whoever doesn't drink with us should meet Perun's bright lightning."

That she did know. When invoking the gods' blessings, it was communion that reached Them, the combined strength of many hearts, many voices, many spirits praying as one. The more gathered together, the likelier the gods were to listen, and she wasn't about to withhold her strength from the communal prayer.

They melded with the crowd, and she craned her neck over their heads, trying to take it all in—the countless blushing faces, the laughs, the widening space from the oaken doorway into what appeared to be an enormous hall.

The ceiling rose high above her, supported by arches made of massive oak trunks, enshrined by walls of carved stone. Vibrant tapestries and a blazing hearth taller than her head made the room feel cozy despite its grand size. Branches of evergreen adorned the eaves and over doorways, and carts of entire hams, sausages, and the most mouth-watering *smalec* bacon spread and boules of rye bread awaited.

The house was much larger on the inside than she had anticipated, and it hummed with voices as the crowd took its place at long tables clothed in white, topped with pitchers of beer and wine, bread and butter, and plates awaiting the household's service of hot food.

As large as the crowd was, there were many more place settings than there were people. So it was the same here as it was at home, where Mama and Mamusia set an extra place at their table in case of a wanderer arriving as a surprise guest. It was said Weles walked the mortal world on this night alone, disguised as a human. Refusing anyone hospitality on the night of Kolęda was to tempt the fury of His demons. No one turned away strangers on this night, nor mistreated them, for they were all Holy Weles.

She followed Stefan as he wended his way through the throng to the very head of the room, where a grand table faced the hall like the moon overlooked the night. Along with his mother, his father, and two other men, Kaspian sat up there with his arms crossed and his eyebrows drawn, his light-blond hair instantly familiar.

He wore a finely tailored coat of evergreen, the wool an expensive close weave, perfectly matched to a luxurious gold trim. His collar, unbuttoned at the neck, teased a peek of an immaculate white shirt. Her fingers twitched at her side, brushing a phantom of its cloth, but she flattened her daydreaming hands to her sides.

It suited him, complementing his large but lean frame, broad shoulders and strong arms tapering to narrow hips. His blond hair, against the forest-green coat's contrast, shone a vibrant wheat-field gold, making it difficult to look away from the handsome face it framed. He was a shining facet of Perun come to earth, and she was the beast gawking at his deific visage.

As Kaspian's cornflower-blue eyes met hers, they widened brightly.

Caught staring. Worse, her mouth hung open, but she still had the wherewithal to close it as he rose and approached her.

"You're here," he called, his deep voice lilting with cheer. Her cheeks heated.

"Yes, I... am," she stammered, although as she watched his face, she couldn't be certain what she'd just said.

As he came to a stop before her, his hands moved to embrace her but stopped just short. She'd held those large, strong hands more than a few times in the past few weeks, tracing the callused patterns of his palms, wondering how his arms would feel around her again. Once, when the rusałki had almost taken him, she'd embraced him on the lake's bank, had felt his chest against hers, but it had been a moment stolen in worry and fear, and had yet to recur.

That recurrence probably shouldn't happen in a hall full of wary villagers.

Clearing his throat, Kaspian clasped his hands behind his back. "I'm sorry I couldn't greet you sooner," he said, his voice dropping as he cast a pointed look in his mother's direction at the table. "I was delayed, unfortunately, but please come, sit."

"Good to see you, too," Stefan murmured, earning an amused tilt of the head and a smirk from Kaspian.

"What? You're here, Stefan? I didn't notice." His eyes sparkling, Kaspian glanced at her and winked before giving Stefan a friendly nudge on the shoulder with his fist.

"You wouldn't. Fairly certain you wouldn't notice a bonfire lighting your backside if Brygida were standing next to it." Stefan stuck out his tongue, while she shifted from foot to foot. They had to be joking. Here, among all these richly clothed carolers, she looked like a wild animal that had stolen in through the back door. And it would be very difficult not to notice a bonfire lighting one's backside.

Kaspian held out a welcoming arm to her and nodded toward the high table.

Glaring at her was Lady Rubin, a jewel made flesh in an intricately embroidered poppy-red dress, looking like a butterfly to her moth. The men sitting with her, Kaspian's father and the two others, were no less decorated, in vividly colored fine fabrics trimmed in cloth of gold.

She rolled her shoulders in her bear fur and eyed Stefan standing next to her. His gaze indicated the high table, and he nodded subtly.

No help there. She glanced toward the crowd, some

of whom looked her over and whispered behind their hands.

Kaspian had mentioned things were strained at home. Would sitting there beside him upset Lady and Lord Rubin?

Warmth embraced her hand—Kaspian's gentle touch. Her breath caught.

"Please," he said kindly, "you're my guest of honor."

His eyes were soft, holding her gaze as warmly as he held her hand, with a fondness they often shared in the quiet serenity of the lake some days. How could she deny those eyes, *him*? This request, or... or *anything* for that matter?

She lurched forward as Stefan gave her a good-natured push.

"You two lovebirds enjoy the den of wolves," he mumbled. "I saw juniper sausage on the way in, and it's calling my name." Grinning, he headed for the long tables.

So he was abandoning them to the mercy of Lady Rubin and her guests.

Entwining her arm around his, Kaspian led her up to the table, where he helped her out of the bear fur and took her headdress before handing them word-lessly to a person behind him.

In the bear fur, she'd stood out like a leg from a pocket, and yet beneath it, her one good dress made her feel naked. A linen dress of the Mrok violet, lined with a ramsthorn-bark brown, it had taken her months to weave and dye the fabric, sew and embroider, and it was the single most luxurious thing she owned. And yet here, among Kaspian's bedecked family and distinguished guests, she looked like a sack of barley.

Summoning the last dregs of her courage, she cleared her throat. "Holy Weles bless you with health, good fortune, and prosperity," she greeted, inclining her head to those already seated.

Lady Rubin huffed with barely a nod, while Lord Rubin exchanged a proper greeting, albeit stiffly.

The man beside Lady Rubin watched her with one eyebrow tilted upward—the well-dressed man Dariusz had been speaking with at the bonfire. She'd never met him before, and despite that first impression with Dariusz of all people, he returned her greeting with the ghost of a smile.

"Oskar Grobowski," he said amiably. "I've been honored with a place at this table as I visit from Granat."

Granat was a region that neighbored Rubin. He'd come quite far. "My name is Bry—"

"Oh, Oskar," Lady Rubin said with an effusive laugh. "You're being quite modest. You're the Lord of Granat. Everyone of worth knows who you are already."

Stung, Brygida looked away, trying to suppress the shudder creeping up her spine.

"Mama," Kaspian growled quietly, glowering at her

as she shrugged a shoulder dismissively and continued chatting with Lord Granat. He glared at the back of Lady Rubin's head before turning back to her, the momentary storm passing.

"What did you think of the ceremony, Brygida?" His blue eyes sparkled, his gaze resting on her face and remaining, as if there were nothing else in the hall. Perhaps he tried to comfort her after the awkwardness with his mother. A valiant effort, and one she'd acknowledge. "I hope it wasn't too boring."

There were things she'd never before seen, ones she'd think about tonight and tomorrow and remember for the rest of her life. "It was beautiful, everyone together celebrating Kolęda. I've never seen anything like it."

"It's rather fun, everyone play-acting..." His gaze flickered toward the person taking away her fur and headdress. "Your costume was stunning. An interpretation of the lejiń?"

She nodded. "On our witchlands, we disguise ourselves as demons to keep the real ones at bay during the rites and to chase away the winter."

He took a deep breath and released it slowly, thoughtfully. "Perhaps our traditions started that way too, before the meaning diluted over the generations."

"Demons are far too frightening for children," Lady Rubin added. "We... appreciate the old ways, but we have to think of the community."

Brygida stiffened. So by wearing the lejiń costume, had she seemed thoughtless about the community?

"You worry too much, Sabina," another man at the table remarked, waving her off.

His voice was the same as the old man's at the bonfire, but his face—

"It's me," he provided with a grin. "Andrzej Wolski, Łukasz's younger, jollier brother," he offered, with a wink for Lord Rubin, who grunted before drinking his wine. "I don't do much around here, but I never miss an opportunity to dress up as Weles and poke a fire with a stick."

Andrzej had a kind face, with a handsomeness that had aged well, and more than a passing resemblance to Kaspian. His shoulder-length hair straddled the boundary between blond and white, however, a mark of his advanced age. The lines of his mouth and the crinkling around his bright blue eyes didn't hide the happy life he must've lived.

"Stryjek Andrzej travels all of Nizina as a storyteller, scholar, and poet," Kaspian said, with more than a little wistfulness. In the time she'd known him, he'd never made it a secret that he chafed against the bonds of his station, and it was clear that his passion lay in art, not rulership. Perhaps his stryjek had been a role model to him?

Before she could reply, the first course was served, roasted mackerel with cloves of garlic, pickled beets with horseradish, and a mix of baked root vegetables with fragrant dill. Her mouth watered as she savored the first bite, but as her skin began to crawl, the mouthful soured.

She was being watched.

The villagers at the long tables kept stealing glances toward her. When she'd been acting as Mokosza's Reaper of Death, they had looked with awe and fear. Now their gazes felt more hostile, more accusatory.

And here, sitting at the high table, offered no concealment, no way to hide. Open and exposed. Was she eating with the correct utensil? Did she keep her mouth closed? Where was she supposed to look, at the plate or...?

By the time the second course came around, she was too self-conscious to eat.

Kaspian leaned in. "Do you not like it?" he asked, his voice an intimate whisper.

"No, it's delicious." She didn't want to seem ungrateful and instead tried to take a few bites. *Pretend they're not there. Pretend they're looking somewhere else. Pretend you're somewhere else...*

Stealing glances at the others seated at the high table, she looked for their utensils, matching them to her own. Lord Granat's eyes met hers, and he offered her a sympathetic smile, raising his fork just high enough that she could clearly see which one it was.

When her gaze met Andrzej's, he pointed at the pickled beets with horseradish and wrinkled his nose.

Next to her, Kaspian raised an eyebrow at him, took a bite, and then quickly reddened. Perhaps the kitchen had been a bit heavy on the horseradish.

As he gulped down his wine, his face still hopelessly red, she suppressed a laugh, catching a bit of escaping mackerel in her palm. Lady Rubin scowled at her, her eyes quickly darting to the myriad long tables, scanning the crowd. Was she afraid they'd seen?

Clearing her throat, Brygida lowered her gaze, resting her hands in her lap. Lady Rubin was right— without even thinking, someone like her could embarrass Kaspian and his entire family.

By the time the desserts came, she was tapping her foot beneath the table, restless, full of unease. This couldn't end fast enough. This space was too open, too exposed, too cramped with eyes and bodies and breaths, packing in, staring, whispering, pointing, judging—

Oaks. She took a deep, cleansing breath, picturing the forest. Black currant brambles, dusted with snow. Boughs heavy with it. A pristine woodscape, quiet and still and tranquil...

Maybe she and Kaspian could be somewhere alone, away from prying eyes, and trade Kolęda blessings.

At last, the plates were cleared away, and as they were, a hush fell over the crowd.

Lord Rubin stood, the lines of his face tightening, and the hearth behind him cast the dark circles beneath his sunken eyes into relief. "Another year comes to an end. We thank you all for the parts you've played to make our village prosper. Now we shall see what fate Weles has in store for each of us in the coming year."

Hadn't they done that at the bonfire? Or was this another divination?

A villager approached with a bundle of hay and handed it to Lord Rubin. He accepted it and stepped down in front of the high table.

The well-dressed Lord Granat sitting beside Lady Rubin stood and walked up to Lord Rubin, who offered the fistful of hay to him.

Lord Granat drew out a piece, a long and straight one ripe with seeds. He turned to show it to the crowd, who clapped as he marched over the hearth and tossed it inside.

What was the meaning of this? Lady Rubin went next, then Kaspian, each drawing a piece, long and straight green ones, and throwing them into the fire.

The villagers lined up to participate as well, while Kaspian rejoined Brygida.

"Don't you want to know what the future holds for you?" he asked her with a smile.

"I've never seen fortunes divined this way," she replied.

"It's simple. You draw a piece of straw and cast it into the fire for Weles, to show your gratitude. The look of the straw tells your fate for the upcoming year. If it's green, it means health. Aa stalk with seeds is abundance. A dry piece means illness. And a broken one... Well, just hope you don't get a broken one."

"What does a broken one signify?" The hairs on the back of her neck stood on end.

"It means death."

Her life had always been steeped in symbols and prophecy, and although this ritual was unfamiliar to her, even the most mundane acts held their own sort of magic. To participate might tempt fate, but to deny it was an insult to the gods.

There was no choice.

She got in line after the villagers. They each took their turns with varying results, each one tossing their lots into the fire, accepting Weles's will.

And then it was her turn.

Lord Rubin hacked a cough as she approached. She'd heard that sort of deep, wet cough before, and it wasn't a good sign. He had to be standing by sheer force of will. He should be abed, resting.

With a tentative hand, she closed her fingers around a piece of hay and slowly drew it out.

Her hand slowly unfurled.

A broken piece.

Death? No.

She couldn't cast this in the fire, couldn't accept it, not—

The doors to the hall slammed open. A cold wind blew, howling ominously.

Lord Rubin's eyes widened. With a wheeze, he collapsed onto the floor before her.

She knelt down beside him as someone screamed and pushed her aside.

"What have you done?" Lady Rubin shoved her backward, but someone caught her shoulders. Kaspian.

"Mama!" he scolded, his voice booming.

"I never should have permitted you here! Get out!" Lady Rubin snapped.

Brygida's mouth dropped open.

Refusing anyone hospitality on Kolęda was to tempt the fury of demons. For Kaspian's mother's sake, she had to—

With a growing susurrus, the villagers closed in, whispering and gasping their shock, pointing fingers at her. Accusations came, one after another.

"No!" Kaspian shouted to the encroaching crowd, rising. "This has nothing to do with Brygida. My father is—"

"Kaspian," Lady Rubin bit out loudly, staring at her icily. "Get *her* away from us this instant."

No matter what scourge Lady Rubin had called down upon herself, staying here in this place, with the anger of the crowd rising, building to bloodshed, would be just as reckless.

Without a word, Brygida rose, twisted out of Kaspian's grip, and fled out into the night, the short, broken piece of hay still clutched in her hand.

This ill omen, linked to another by Lady Rubin's refusal of hospitality—if she didn't do something to appease Weles, what fate would befall them both?

CHAPTER 4

Tonight couldn't have gone more wrong.

Kaspian paced the length of his parents' chambers. The stifling air stank of musty medicinal herbs. Thick blankets and goose-down pillows consumed Tata's shrunken and pale body. The healer at his bedside, backlit by the fireplace, cast a dark shadow over him like the looming presence of Weles waiting to spirit him to the world below.

When Kaspian had been a boy, Tata had seemed like the perfect masterpiece: a man who had everything —a loving wife, two healthy sons, and rulership of a prosperous region. Now, his body shriveled by illness and eyes scrunched, he seemed more like a crumpled sketch.

As angry as he'd been with both of his parents, he couldn't be so cold as to abandon Tata in his time of need. When Tata had collapsed, the only thought in his head had been: *Don't let him be dead.*

Each of Tata's breaths threatened to be a death rattle, punctuated by a hacking cough and the deepening furrows of his face. The sickness had stolen so much from him, leaving his skin paper thin, nearly translucent, the blue veins streaks against snowy white flesh stretched over all-too-conspicuous bones.

The healer released a heavy sigh as she turned away from Tata.

"How is he?" Even through the hand rubbing his face, Kaspian still couldn't keep the tremor from his voice.

Her kind eyes met his. "He needs rest." She turned away as if to leave.

"But he's going to get better, right?" He touched her elbow.

She yanked it backward, her eyes wide.

He stepped back from her, nearly colliding with Mama's writing desk. It hadn't been his intention to frighten her; what was it about the casual touch that had done so?

The healer's eyes darted toward the door.

"I'm sorry. I didn't mean to alarm you." Although his muscles were tense, he kept his arms at his side and tried to look as non-threatening as possible.

She licked her lips, her taut shoulders slackening a

bit. "There's nothing else I can do. His illness has progressed too far."

The ground sank beneath him. He collapsed into Mama's chair, his head in his hands.

This couldn't be happening. Tata couldn't die.

"There must be something that can be done?" he pleaded. He didn't care if he looked like a fool. He wasn't about to let Tata die.

She shook her head. "There's nothing. I'm sorry."

After gathering up her things, she headed for the door.

The fireplace crackled, and Tata coughed, his frail body convulsing amid layers of linen, wool, and heavy down. Over time, his body had become smaller and smaller, like a figure fading into the distance.

He wouldn't let Tata fade away. Not if he could help it.

There were healers in other villages, perhaps more skilled, who could find ways to extend his life. But this late in the winter, travelling was difficult and slow. The chances were high he'd return with a healer only for Tata to have passed in the interim.

His eyes burned, and he wiped at them. "Tata, you can't leave us."

The frail hand resting upon the covers had once handed him a practice sword when he'd been a little boy, sending him to the weaponmaster. *Your brother will be lord when I die. But you must always be prepared to fight for your blood.*

Kaspian closed his fingers around a phantom sword. Tata had always reinforced the lesson. Now, more than ever, he wanted to fight for his blood, for his father, and that want paced inside of him like a caged animal. There was no sword that could cure what ailed Tata, and the sword-arm that had prepared to fight for his blood was useless here.

There was a knock at the door, and Kaspian's head shot up. A maid entered with more firewood. She headed straight for the fireplace, with one quick glance toward the bed where Tata lay before lowering her chin sadly.

He refused to believe there was nothing to be done. The healer had acted strangely; there must be another explanation.

"The healer who was here, do you know her?" Kaspian asked.

The maid shook her head. "Not well, my lord."

"Is it possible she might have some grudge against us? Have you heard anything?"

The maid wrung her hands together, avoiding his eyes. "I'm not sure."

He stood and took a step toward her. Her gaze wavered.

"If there's something you know, please tell me. My father's life is at stake."

She stared at the floor, fidgeting with her apron. "It's nonsense, but..."

"But what?"

"There... there are some who believe you framed Julian by paying the witches to punish the wrong man."

His gut twisted. Did some of the villagers still suspect him even when the real culprit had been caught? What would the witches even do with all the coin? They didn't even leave their forest, much less frequent the village and buy lavish things.

But if these rumors were spreading, could that mean the healer wasn't properly treating Tata because of him?

"I don't believe such things," she quickly added. "But it is being said."

Tata mumbled something incoherent, and Kaspian's head popped up.

Taking a seat at the edge of the bed, he grasped Tata's withered hand. Blinded by resentment, he'd deluded himself into thinking it hadn't been as bad as Tata had feared, that he would get better.

His throat constricted. Losing Roksana had been hard enough, and losing Tata as well, with everything left unresolved? It would only get worse. Knowing death was coming didn't make it any easier to process. He stroked Tata's knuckles with his thumb. These strong hands had once picked him up to ride on his shoulders, had swung him around to his delightful squeals.

Tata's fingers curled around his. There was hardly any strength in them, just the barest brush against his skin. Tata inhaled, his voice raspy, and Kaspian leaned in to hear him.

"What is it, Tata?"

"Sabina." Tata said Mama's name like a sigh.

Where was Mama? He'd been so concerned with Tata's health, he hadn't even realized she wasn't at Tata's side. She should be here.

It was understandable that she'd remained behind to calm the crowd after that disastrous offering, and to charm Lord Granat, who surely had questions. If he hadn't known about Tata's condition before, he knew now. It was fortunate that Mama was a skilled diplomat —Tata's collapse only made the situation more complicated.

But enough time had passed for all that, and she should be here. Perhaps Lord Granat had detained her?

Kaspian massaged his aching temples. He was out of his depth here. As much as he despised Lord Granat and shouldn't speak to him right now, he should probably intervene, for Tata's sake.

He squeezed Tata's hand. "I will find her. Don't worry."

Tata's hand slipped through his fingers, falling onto the bed limply as another violent cough shuddered through him. Each one felt like a dagger to his own chest.

"Stay with him until I return with my mother," Kaspian said to the maid. Once she nodded, he slid out into the hall.

Outside the door, the din of voices reached even up here. The entire manor was alive and restless. As he reached the bottom of the steps, he had to brace himself on the stone wall. His hands shook.

He'd been trying to put the people and the rulership first, but everything was crumbling around him. Tata was dying, whether they reconciled their differences or not. Roksana was gone, no matter what he thought he should have done.

And Brygida... He'd wanted tonight to be perfect; instead, it had been a perfect disaster. Had he managed to change some minds with his words? Surely everyone could understand that Tata's collapse had just been a coincidence.

Had she made it home safely? When she'd run out, he'd wanted to chase after her, but Tata had needed him more. And now, there was nothing more he could do. There was no subverting fate, but try as he might to hold on, each of its turns climbed over him like fractals of frost, burdening him more and more heavily like so much ice.

With his tenuous control beginning to weaken, he took a fortifying breath. He couldn't face the servants and peasants like this. No, he needed a drink to steel his nerves enough to get through the rest of the night. He pressed his head against the smooth stone wall. It cooled his fevered brow.

"And what about your daughter?" Mama asked, her voice echoing off the stone.

"She is displeased, but it is not her decision. It is mine," Lord Granat's deep baritone rumbled.

Kaspian straightened, pressing his back against the wall that joined the stairway and the solarium. What was it that displeased Lord Granat's daughter, the so-called Bear of Granat?

Rumor had it she was beastly in appearance, with a nose that dominated her face and ears big enough to take flight. If that wasn't bad enough, they said her temper matched her looks. Whispers from travelers who stopped in Rubin said that those who crossed her rarely got away unscathed. Last spring, after Lord Granat had married his son to Lord Bursztyn's daughter, a travelling merchant had told Kaspian that the Bear of Granat had poisoned her brother in a jealous rage, and it had left him sickly and impotent.

Tata lay dying in his bed, and Mama was making idle conversation? He should make his presence known.

"The children will have to understand. We're only doing what's best for them," Mama said.

The *children*. That was why Lord Granat had come

here in the dead of winter. His mother would try to betroth him to the Bear of Granat.

For all her protests about Brygida, Mama intended to sidestep them all by manipulating him into marriage to the Bear of Granat.

Over his dead body. He'd thwart it in every way possible until he became lord, and after that, her manipulations would no longer matter.

"Sabina, I don't know what I would do without you." Lord Granat's voice dropped an octave lower. It was perversely intimate.

Kaspian's fingers curled into a fist, but he didn't move. Tata was on his deathbed, and Lord Granat made overtures to Mama? She would tell this boor where to go.

"Oh, Oskar." Mama's trill of laughter echoed around him.

What? He had to have heard that wrong, but it sounded genuine. Perhaps it was part of her strategy?

As he peeked around the corner, Lord Granat had his back to him with Mama facing him, smiling. Not her forced diplomat's smile. The beaming smile he hadn't seen in months. Her hand rested on Lord Granat's arm.

A vein in his jaw twitched. He bit down on the expletives that threatened to burst from him. While his father lay dying, she was flirting with this tyrant? Arranging another betrothal to a woman who'd likely kill him on their wedding night? Perun's bright lightning, he hoped it wasn't true, but she could be cold and calculating.

Mama's eyes met his and widened. She jerked her hand away. "Kaspian, I was just—"

"Tata is asking for you," he bit out as he approached them. There was no use in hiding now.

Lord Granat turned to face him, his thick sandy-blond eyebrows shadowing dark eyes that stared him down.

"I hope Lord Rubin is recuperating." Those dark, shrewd eyes sized him up. There was a challenge in that gaze, a desire to snatch these last scraps of power and wealth from a dying man's hand.

"This was nothing. He's strong and will be back to his old self in no time," Kaspian said, forcing a confidence he didn't feel. Then to Mama, he said, "Mama, what were you tending to here that's more important than your husband?" he asked through clenched teeth.

The palest rosy blush reddened the bridge of her nose and cheeks.

"Is that any way to speak to your mother?" Lord Granat growled.

Lord Granat should know. He'd certainly spoken to a married woman, the wife of his host, in a way that had exceeded all bounds of propriety just now.

"This is a family matter," Kaspian replied, with thinly veiled venom.

Mama gasped. Lord Granat's bushy brows drew into a line, but he made no further comment.

"Kaspian, don't be rude to our guest. We... I... Forgive my son." Her gaze flitted to Lord Granat's as she stammered for words. If this was some diplomatic ploy, it was utterly unlike her.

"Tata has been asking for you," he added bitterly. "But if you'd rather play hostess, I shall leave you to it."

"Excuse me, Oskar, but my family needs me." Her face downcast, she pulled away.

Blood surged through his veins like boiling water, and his breaths were quick, harsh.

As she began to make her way toward the stairs, he spun on his heel and strode away from them. His body wanted a fight, even as he schooled his legs to take him as far from Lord Granat's punch-worthy face as possible. And there was no way he could be in a room with Mama without demanding answers, and right now, Tata's well-being was paramount.

It was preposterous, seeing her smiling, laughing, while Tata was dying. He balled his hand into a fist. Did she not care at all? Was the affectionate, doting mother he'd known a lie as well, just as Henryk, the perfect older brother, had been a lie? He took a ragged breath, tugging at his coat's cuffs, then dragged a hand over his face. He pulled at the buttons of his collar and undid the first three.

He needed to get out of here, get some air, calm

down. Let Tata have the time he'd asked for with his wife.

Peasants lingered in the corridors, muttering amongst themselves in clustered groups. As he approached, they parted, observing him, some with concerned eyes and others with suspicious glances. How many among them believed the rumors? Who had spread such malicious lies about him, and how could he stop it?

Out in the yard, the bonfire flickered against the indigo sky, where stray sparks carried on the wind like false stars. Long shadows crept beside the buildings and obscured the faces of those who'd remained behind, drinking and talking. There was no merry dancing or joyous expectation of a new year ahead. A shroud had been cast over the village.

Snow flurried around him as his boots crunched on hard-packed ice, flattened by the feet of many peasants coming to the manor. Without gloves, his fingers tingled from the cold. Flexing and blowing on them to keep warm, he proceeded along the road. Cloaked in midnight, he walked without destination, hoping only to let the heat of his anger chill in the frigid air.

His fingers started to ache and he couldn't stop shivering, but still he trudged forward. The night was still, and the clouds moved lazily across the sky, revealing a full moon that cast the landscape in silver. An ancient barren oak, its skeletal branches blanketed in snow, towered menacingly over the crossroads. Time and time again his feet had guided him back here, to the Perun-struck oak, as if returning here could change the past.

The last place he'd seen Roksana.

Over and over he had wondered: what would his life have been like had he walked her to her door that night? They'd have been wed and Tata would still be dying, but the illusion of his perfect family would have remained intact. Perhaps he could have learned to love her, as she'd said.

But what of Brygida? Would she have been in the woods with her mothers tonight, free of fear? Her life unchanged and unthreatened by the mistrust of the peasants?

Had they not had that one chance encounter in the woods, would Roksana still be alive?

But if not for Roksana's death, would he now know Brygida so well?

It was impossible to know, all of it.

The time he'd spent with Brygida meant more than all the gold in Tata's coffers. At times it felt like a dream, one he would wake from all too soon. If he could, he would give up everything to make sure he never did wake from it.

"Kaspian?" Brygida's voice came to him as if he were indeed in a waking dream.

But as he glanced back, she really was there, shivering. The tip of her nose was red with cold, and her hair was in wild strands. Her bear fur and headdress were nowhere to be found, and she wore only her violet dress.

His stomach fluttered. Even knowing how dangerous it was for her to be here while the peasants were so restless, he was glad to see her. Greedy, wretched man that he was.

He unbuttoned his coat, and her gaze followed his descending hands, lower and lower and lower.

"What are you doing here?" he asked too loudly, his bewildered voice shattering the silence of the winter night.

She huffed a laugh, a cloud of vapor rising from her pink lips. "I saw you in the distance and followed you here."

"But I thought Stefan escorted you home." He shed his coat and wrapped it around her shoulders before she could object. It practically swallowed her whole.

"I can walk myself home. But I did decide to pay Demon a visit before heading back," she said with a smile, nuzzling her cheek against his coat's collar.

Even with everything in his life collapsing right now, Perun's bright lightning, he'd never wanted to be anything as much as he wanted to be a coat in this moment.

"We should talk about what happened at the manor," she said softly.

"Maybe not just yet?" It was self-indulgent of him,

perhaps, to want to live in this moment a little longer, but he did. Tonight should have been perfect, but it had all fallen apart. Even if the festival had gone wrong, maybe he could salvage these last few moments of the evening with her. Just one bright moment, a spark against the gloom.

She grasped his hand, and his entire body froze. It wasn't like her to touch him so forwardly.

"Why did you go out into the cold without gloves?" She wrapped his hand in both of hers, rubbing them together, awakening warmth back in his fingers.

"Perhaps precisely for this reason." He tried to smile.

She raised her eyebrow, huffed another laugh, and then took his other hand, repeating what she'd done with the first.

"Thank you for the coat, but I'll walk you home before you freeze to death," she said, giving his arm a tug.

"It should be me." His heart ached as the ghost of Roksana flared to life once more in his memory.

"Why is that? The manor is much closer, and you'll lose a finger if you go to the cottage and back."

He coughed to cover up a laugh. He wasn't sure if he should explain it or just leave it be. She didn't need to be walked home. She wasn't Roksana. Sometimes he forgot that. "Perhaps I want to spend a little more time with you?"

"Oh." A rosy pink flushed across her face. "Come. I'll lend you a cloak from the cottage."

They turned their steps toward the forest. Snow crunched under their booted feet, but there was no other sound. Although he was shivering, he didn't want to hurry home, so he dragged each footfall.

As they walked, her fingers grazed his again. Would it be too presumptuous to try to hold her hand under the pretense of keeping warm? It wasn't like they'd never done it before. These casual touches lit something in him, a burning that grew hotter the longer they were together. It warmed him more than any coat or glove could.

When they'd been children, Roksana had always insisted they hold hands when it was cold like this. A lump formed in his throat, and he withdrew his hand so it wouldn't accidentally brush Brygida's again. He should be loving this, every second of it, but his mind was elsewhere and everything else felt dulled, like a canvas painted with diluted watercolors.

"How is your father?" Brygida asked.

He winced, a shudder rippling through him, then froze in place. It seemed they couldn't avoid the grim events of tonight any longer.

"The healer says he's dying." He swallowed past the lump in his throat. "I don't know what to do." He heaved a sigh, a cloud of vapor shrouding his face.

She reached up and grasped his shoulder, pulling

him down into her embrace. Other than when she'd hugged him by the lake, when he'd nearly died, they'd never embraced this way. It felt warm and right, and the comfort was exactly what he needed right now. He let out another shaking breath. He didn't want to cry, not in front of her, but his eyes watered as thick puffs of white air escaped with each ragged breath.

"I don't want my father to die," he confessed, whispering to her hoarsely.

She held him closer, nodding against his neck. "Mama is the best healer I know. Maybe there's something she can do." She bit her lip.

Was there? If Ewa could be persuaded, maybe Tata would have a chance?

He withdrew, only enough to see her face fully, her violet eyes reflecting a spectral silver in the moonlight. "Are you sure? After all my family has done, I wouldn't expect her help."

Looking away, Brygida wouldn't meet his gaze, staring down at their feet. "She's just trying to protect me. I'll talk to her. I'm sure there's something that can be done."

It was a chance. The smallest sliver of one, but it was all he had.

CHAPTER 5

Normally home was a welcome sight, but as the warm golden light cast from the cottage's frosted windows, the knot in Brygida's chest didn't loosen. The broken piece of hay stabbed her through the fabric of her dress, where it was hidden. A death omen, Lord Rubin's collapse, and Mamusia's warning all whirled in her head. And now she had to somehow convince Mama to treat a dying man.

Why had she lied to Kaspian? Even Mama, as skilled a healer as she was, couldn't stop Weles's summons. But he'd just appeared so defeated, and she had to help. Besides, village medicine was often far behind theirs. It was worth the attempt to delay the inevitable, wasn't it?

As she reached for the handle, Mama's and Mamusia's voices drifted from beyond the door as they often did. But an unfamiliar third joined them. A visitor? Now? Perhaps one of the village women had come for a remedy.

When she opened the door, a blanket of warmth hit her frigid face, and she was greeted by the smoky scent of a crackling fire. Mamusia took the kettle off the hook, while Mama and a young woman sat at the table together.

"Welcome home," Mamusia said with an airy lightness as she filled four cups on the table. They'd been expecting her. "How was the celebration?"

The less was said about that, the better. Before Kaspian could get too far from the cottage, she grabbed her hooded rabbit-fur cloak and ran back out the door. Kaspian would freeze if he had to walk home in just his shirt, and even his own coat that he'd lent to her wouldn't be enough. She wouldn't have him losing a finger.

"Kaspian!" she called out, her booted feet sinking in the snow as she followed her own tracks backward.

A lone figure paused along the deer path. "Brygida? Is everything all—"

She jogged up to him, holding out the rabbit fur. "I still need to speak to Mama and convince her, but if she agrees, we'll be there as soon as we can. In the meantime, take this. It's warm and should keep you alive until you're back at the manor," she offered with a smile.

"And then?" He eyed the grooved gray fur before meandering a look to her face, his mouth turning up slightly. Of course she cared about his health, if that was the reason for his amusement?

Her cheeks burned, probably from the cold. As he accepted the fur, she cleared her throat and then fled, a soft chuckle fading behind her. She glanced back, watching him as he donned the fur over broad shoulders and pulled the hood up over his blond head. The cloak was too short on him, naturally, but it would keep him warm enough.

He raised a hand in parting, and she did the same, her blasted cheeks heating once more. She returned to the cottage, facing three sets of staring eyes.

Mama's sharp green gaze fixed on her, but Mamusia breezed into her line of sight, holding out tea. Biting her lip, Brygida quickly kicked the snow off her boots and accepted the cup gratefully, letting it warm her hands. The rosehip scent was comforting and familiar.

Their guest's auburn hair was bound in a thick braid, her willowy body clad in wool, with leathers and a bow resting on the table. Her face was all devastating planes and angles, and there was a sharpness to her green eyes that reminded her very much of Mama. But there were eagles with softer expressions than this stranger.

"Who's our guest?" Brygida asked.

"Halina. She's a huntress from my old coven," Mama said warmly.

Bowing her head, Halina sketched a smile.

If she was a witch of the Huntresses of Dziewanna, then she was family. "Nice to meet you. What brings you to us in this weather?"

Halina eyed her bow and lowered her chin gravely. "I've been tracking a demon through the countryside."

A chill swept down her spine. Red eyes in the forest. Mamusia's premonition had come true in reality. Brygida's hand brushed across where the broken straw lay hidden in the folds of her dress. Death. That was what the broken piece meant, didn't it?

"A demon? But shouldn't we be safe on our witchlands?" Brygida grabbed her vial of lake water hanging at her neck. She hadn't met a demon yet that could withstand the wrath of the blood, not here where she and her mothers were most powerful.

"We should." Mama frowned, rapping her fingers on the table nervously. It was a rare thing to see Mama unsettled by anything. What made her doubt their safety?

Halina fidgeted with the end of her braid, exchanging a look with Mama. "You should be safe on your witchlands... For now."

For now? Should she run out and warn Kaspian? She looked at the door.

Mama glared at Halina, who dropped her gaze to the table, chastised.

Brygida canted her head. Mama had never used that glare on anyone else besides her. Mama had said that before she'd met Mamusia, she'd been a high-ranking huntress among her coven. Even now, after years away, did she still hold the same authority?

Halina cleared her throat. "Before you arrived, I was telling Ewa about the rise of demon sightings." Her gaze shifted to Mama once more, and Mama shook her head slightly, almost imperceptibly. "I am hunting a demon that led me here to your witchlands. Until I kill it, it would be inadvisable to go out into the forest, or else I cannot be held responsible for the consequences."

The broken straw scratched against her skin. All of this couldn't be a mere coincidence.

"Enough of this gloomy talk." Flashing a stern violet gaze at Mama, Mamusia joined them at the table with a plate of sweet, crisp *faworki*. "Brygida, how was the village celebration?"

She bit her lip. If she told them the truth, they might never let her go out into the village again. But she'd promised Kaspian she would ask Mama for help.

"It was... nice. The celebration is different," she answered, and Mamusia wrinkled her nose.

"You were among the villagers?" Halina stared blankly at Mama. "Are you certain that's wise?"

"It wasn't my choice," Mama said, crossing her arms over her chest.

"But?" Mamusia prompted, ignoring them both. She nodded an invitation to continue.

Brygida cleared her throat. "Well, Lord Rubin has been ill for a while, and... he collapsed." She looked at Mama, who in turn avoided her gaze, looking everywhere around the cottage but at her.

There was no sense in dancing around the question, and no time. She squirmed, trying to find her voice again. This wasn't going to be easy, but it was now or never. "I was hoping... Well... Mama, would you please come with me and see if you could help him?"

Mama raised an eyebrow as she regarded her. "After all the ill that man has done, you would want me to heal him? I say good riddance," she spat.

"Ewa," Mamusia scolded, nudging her arm.

"What has he done?" A sharp accusation hardened Halina's tone. Her eyes so keenly fixed on her bow they practically reached for it.

"Nothing like that," Brygida said quickly. "I can admit he's made mistakes, but that doesn't mean he deserves to die."

"It was not I who condemned him." Rearranging her skirts, Mama stood and walked over to the fire, stoking the embers. The flames rose higher.

Mama was stubborn, but she had to do something.

Even if she could only extend his life a short while, wouldn't that be enough?

"Please, Mama?" she pleaded. "I made a promise to Kaspian."

With an exasperated huff, Mama snapped a glare over her shoulder. "Don't think you can sway me with promises you made to him. If I had my way, you'd never see him again." She turned back to the fire and fiercely prodded it some more.

"But she's right, Ewa," Mamusia said, pulling her shawl closer. "He's a parent after all, and what he did was to protect his child. Wouldn't you have done the same for Brygida if you'd believed she was innocent?"

A sniff. "That is completely different. You know what his older son did."

"And we also jumped to conclusions to condemn his younger son," Mamusia replied quietly, some ghost stirring in her gaze.

What had gotten into Mamusia lately? Did she regret what they'd almost done to Kaspian? Was this her way of atoning?

Whatever it was, Mama softened at Mamusia's words, lowering her hands from her hips and taking a deep, cleansing breath. "Liliana, you'll be the death of me," she said with a sigh. "I'll go and see Lord Rubin, but only on one condition."

"Anything," Brygida said eagerly, sitting on the edge of her chair.

Mama turned to her, arms crossed, pinning her with a no-nonsense look. "You promise not to sneak out of the cottage to see that *boy* without my permission."

Mama may as well have told her she could never leave the cottage again—that would be closer to the truth.

But she'd made a promise to Kaspian, and his father's life was at stake. Besides, agreeing to this condition didn't mean things would never change.

With a little luck and hopefully Mokosza's own hand, Mama would come around as Mamusia had.

Or at least that was what she'd tell herself. "I agree."

❦

A FLURRY OF SNOW DRIFTED DOWN FROM A SLATE-GRAY sky. Stomping his feet on the icy crust, Kaspian rubbed his arms through his woolen coat as he waited, trying to fight back the cold. He clutched Brygida's rabbit-fur cloak, to return to her of course, but despite his best efforts, nothing could warm him. It was more than skin deep.

After a long and restless night, Tata had not slipped away as he'd feared, but his condition had not improved.

Kaspian tilted his head back, and delicate flakes melted as they hit his flushed skin. As a child, he had tried catching flakes on his tongue with Roksana. They'd run in circles, tongues out. At times, they'd collide into one another before collapsing into giggles in the snow. Those precious memories had been as fleeting as these snowflakes, gone in an instant. A small rivulet of snowmelt rolled down to his chin as he jerked his head down.

The cold had crept in, freezing him from the inside, as if Weles had a wintry grip upon his heart. What if it was too late to save Tata, even with Ewa's intervention?

That was if Brygida could convince Ewa to examine Tata at all. There was no love lost between the witches and his parents.

A bleak wall of clouds hid the sun's position, but it had to be past midday.

Perhaps they weren't coming after all...

Throat tight, he gazed from the crossroads back to the manor. The stone-and-wood building melted into a single monotone horizon, like the murky water he used to rinse a paint brush. Should he turn back? Search out another plan?

For just a bit longer, he'd wait. He wasn't ready to give up yet. Brygida wouldn't let him down.

To keep out the penetrating cold, he paced a furrow in the snow. The farmlands were blanketed in white, an occasional gray stone fence poking through snow banks the only indication of property lines.

Haggard black trees marked the border between the village and the forest, the Perun-struck oak the biggest of them all. Its dead branches reached toward the sky, the charred mark twisting down to its roots. If it weren't for the plumes of smoke rising from the chimneys of the farmhouses, he would have felt he was alone in this lonely and barren landscape.

After making half a dozen passes along the cross-roads, he stopped and stared at the forest. Bare tree limbs dusted with white. In winters past, they'd inspired him to paint. But now everything felt bleached of color, like old bones left in the sun.

Why would Ewa ever agree to see Tata?

If she didn't, the fate of the region would fall upon Kaspian's shoulders sooner than he'd anticipated. He wasn't ready, and it was possible he might never be. Tata had kept the region prosperous and the people safe from famine and other disasters that had plagued their neighbors. Could he do the same?

Amongst the dark silhouettes of the oaks, two cloaked figures emerged. The knot in his chest loosened. She'd convinced Ewa to come. There was hope for Tata.

He waved them over as they trudged their way through the snow-dense fields.

"Thank you for coming. It means the world to me and my family," Kaspian said to Ewa as she approached. He offered her his arm to help her over a snowbank, but she grunted and ignored his gesture.

"We'll see what can be done. I'm not a miracle work-
er." Her lips were pulled thin.

He should have expected a frigid reception from
Ewa, but at least she was here. That was one thing to be
grateful for.

At Ewa's shoulder, Brygida gave him a reassuring
smile. He held out the rabbit-fur cloak, but she was clad
in another, a white one that brushed the ground.
Liliana's? "Oh, I thought you might need—"

"It's all right," she offered brightly, accepting the
cloak. "Thank you."

It was he who should thank her; she'd given him
hope. "I still have your bear fur and headdress
inside—"

Ewa stepped between him and Brygida, spearing
him with a glare.

He cleared his throat and indicated the manor gates.
"Shall we, then?"

This time of year, the servants worked indoors, or
those who tended the animals stayed in warm barns.
The gates were unguarded now. The scattered ashes of
the Kolęda bonfire and the multitude of footprints
had churned the ground into a taupe muck that had
frozen over once more. As the three of them crossed
the yard, their footsteps crunched and frost clung to
their boots.

As they entered the main hall, the heat of the fire
and the merry chatter of the servants gathered inside

greeted them. He stomped his feet to shake off the ice and mud, followed by Ewa and Brygida.

He gestured down the hall. "This way, please."

The conversation hushed, and as they passed, whispered voices overlapped one another. The servants could gossip all they wanted. It didn't matter what they thought, as long as he could save Tata.

Up the stairs and down another hallway, he guided them to Tata and Mama's chamber. The thick, dry air inside smelled of wax from too many candles left burning too long. He shed his cloak, placing it over a nearby chair.

At Tata's bedside, Mama stood from her seat, rearranging her shawl although its drape had already been perfect.

"Kaspian, what is the meaning of this?" Her regal gaze darted to Ewa as she crossed her arms over her chest.

"I brought a healer," he said.

Paying Mama no mind, Ewa pushed back her hood but did not shed her cloak. Clearly she did not plan to stay long. Brygida followed her mother's lead.

Mama straightened her shoulders, her hands clenched into fists at her side. "You should have discussed it with me first," she said to him, as if Ewa and Brygida weren't even in the room.

Tata needed care, and he'd brought it. "Why? What is there to discuss?"

She didn't follow him.

He clenched his hands into fists until they ached. He wasn't sure how long he stood there in the doorway, blind to everything around him, when he felt a gentle hand on his shoulder. Brygida's violet gaze filled his vision.

She didn't need to say anything. Just being close to her soothed the bitterness, anger, and regret. He unclenched his fist and glanced to Tata's sleeping form. Ewa seemed to be finishing up, her deft hands brushing over his head and neck, then lifting his wrist, one thumb pressed against his pulse.

"How is he? Is there anything that can be done?" he asked.

Ewa straightened, and her somber gaze met his. Ice filled his veins.

"I've done all I can. But he only has a week left, at most two if you're lucky."

One week.

Kaspian's knees buckled beneath him. He would have fallen to the ground had Brygida not caught him and guided him to a chair. He clutched his head in his hands.

Tata had one week left to live.

CHAPTER 6

Despite Brygida's protests, Mama nearly dragged her from the manor house. They cut across snow-covered fields, their footsteps pressing deep tracks in the fresh snow, and Mama's grip on her forearm didn't loosen even once. Had she not seen the look of utter defeat on Kaspian's face? He'd been devastated. She'd wanted nothing more than to wrap him in her embrace, provide the same sort of comfort Mama and Mamusia had always given her when she was sad.

She and Mama had an agreement, but that didn't mean abandoning Kaspian in his time of need. "Mama, please, let me stay with him. He's hurting, badly."

"It's not safe among the village right now." Mama scrutinized the farmhouse they passed. "Didn't you see how they looked at us?"

She'd seen, all right. The broken bit of hay remained hidden in her dress, its fate yet undecided. It should have been burned, and she should have surrendered to the will of Weles. Perhaps she still could have given her offering to the fire, after everything. But doing so would have felt too much like proving to the village that she was the reason Lord Rubin had collapsed, the unlucky ill-fated shadow clinging to their lord and his family.

Besides, she couldn't gamble with the offering on a hunch, not when the right answer could be in the Mrok grimoire. She just needed a moment alone to check.

"Something happened on Kolęda, didn't it?" Mama asked quietly, not meeting her eyes.

She wrested free of Mama's grip as they entered a tangled grove of oaks. She should tell the truth, but if she did, that meant never leaving her witchlands or the cottage again. Never seeing Kaspian again. She couldn't do it. "All that happened was Lord Rubin collapsed, just like I told you."

The bitter lies coated her tongue, and Mama strode quickly, ignoring the usual deer path for another, casting a furtive glance behind her.

When had lying to Mama become so easy? A couple months ago, their bond had been strong, and at most, she'd fibbed about watching the villagers or tarrying in her duties to daydream. But now? A rift had begun to widen between them, one she misliked but couldn't seem to close.

When they arrived back at the cottage, Halina was outside, her horse saddled, flicking its tail.

"I was hoping I'd see you before I left," she said soberly to Mama, who approached and traded some quiet conversation.

Brygida slipped into the cottage, where Mamusia hummed as she ground herbs with her pestle. Her eyes brightened a moment in greeting, but she didn't halt her work.

With both Mama and Mamusia distracted, now was the perfect time to learn what to do with her offering. Brygida grabbed the grimoire and took it to her bed, then pulled out the broken hay from its hiding place.

She'd once read in the grimoire that death had multiple meanings. It could be a literal end of life, but it also could mean the end of other things, some part of her life. She thumbed through the pages, searching for a prayer. If the omen meant what she thought, it foretold the end of her freedom, of... her and Kaspian.

No, these past few weeks with Kaspian had been the happiest of her life.

But these types of omens had a way of rippling outwards. The village's hostility toward her, toward her mothers, might only be the beginning. Mama was right —it wasn't safe—and the last thing she wanted was for someone to get hurt, whether it meant one of them or a villager. By not giving the offering to the fire, maybe she could thwart the fate this hay foretold. There had to be a way to appease Weles, to go back to how things had been before Kolęda.

After searching through the grimoire, she found her first promising passage. It was short, describing how an unwanted augury might be changed with a prayer and an offering. There were certain ingredients she needed. And a place of worship, a Mouth of Weles, a deep chasm in the earth. There was one that came to mind, but it was far from the cottage. Getting there unbeknownst to Mama would be tricky.

But it had to be done; perhaps she'd find a way to change her fate. Closing the book, she headed into the main room of the cottage. Outside, Mama and Halina were still talking. From the agitation in Halina's tone, it didn't sound good. But perhaps it would keep Mama occupied long enough. And Mamusia had finished with the pestle and was now knitting in the corner as Brygida sidled over to Mama's supply of herbs.

"Need something?" Mamusia didn't look up from her work.

"Just something for a headache." Brygida grasped for the jar of the herb she needed.

"You're taking motherwort for a headache?" Mamusia asked, her voice lilting and teasing.

Her hand froze reaching for the jar. "Silly me." She reached for the sweet violet leaf.

Mamusia stood and joined her at the herbs, then picked up the jar of motherwort. "This is used for prayers. What could you be praying for, I wonder?"

Her heart leapt into her throat. Did Mamusia suspect?

Mamusia reached for the burnet, the centaury—jars that Brygida needed for the prayer, and placed them in a satchel that she handed to Brygida, with a wink.

"It seems we're out of elm bark. Would you go and fetch some for me?" Mamusia asked airily.

This couldn't be—could it? Mamusia was helping her. It wasn't sneaking out if Mamusia sent her for something, was it?

"Won't Mama be angry?" Brygida asked, raising an eyebrow. She shouldn't protest the assistance, but she didn't want to come between her mothers either.

Mamusia put her hands on her shoulders. "I dreamed again last night. The red eyes in the night wood returned, and there were more of them than before." She shook her head. "Whatever you're praying for, I think it's necessary. Ewa disagrees and believes you must be guarded, and we can't see eye to eye on what to do. But I can feel it, you are critical to stop it."

More red eyes? She drew back, clutching her vial of lake water tightly. But she didn't have time to dwell on the thought.

On Mamusia's request, she'd be leaving the cottage —not sneaking out—and she could find one of Weles's sacred places. She headed out the back while Mama said her goodbyes to Halina.

The winter woods were restless; the oaks creaked, branches reaching outward, twisting together as if to keep something out. Daylight was precious this time of year, and as the afternoon stretched, Halina's warning echoed in her head. She dared not linger a moment longer than necessary. The threat of demons quickened her footsteps, and she made her way to the cavern.

Willows guarded its entrance, the stout earthen sentries of Weles, and she bowed her head to their presence as she entered.

Inside, the air was warmer, more humid, and she pulled back her hood as she ventured deeper. Sunlight filtered in from an opening above, where snowflakes tumbled and icicles dripped, a never-ending beat of water drops resounding against stone walls. The chasm below was partially covered in snow, the craggy rocks at its rim frosted.

Here she prepared her offering. She began with the consecration, preparing a makeshift altar of a crag before the abyss. She lit three candles from her satchel, and from the third a fourth. Holding it high, she circled the chasm. "Holy Dażbóg, Shining Sun, bless this place, I beseech You. Set it aside from the rest of this world, and tether it to the heavens, the home of Your father."

She set the fourth and final candle on the altar, then bound the herbs into incense. Touching it to the fire of each candle, she lit it, spreading its fragrant smoke before her. "Mighty Weles, come to me and receive my gift, I entreat You humbly. Wandering Bear, Wolf of the World Below, Grandfather of Magic and Music, hear my call. Glory to You, Horned Serpent, who fights thunder without fear. Glory to You, Weles."

She wrapped the piece of broken hay in linen and placed it on the altar. "I give this fateful hay to You, Weles. Please accept it."

Holding her arms open in offering, she waited. Melted ice dripped, dripped, dripped. The incense washed over her with its heady herbal scent, singed with the char of the four candles. The wind whispered outside, conversing with the sway of willow branches, then howled through the cavern. It whipped against her hood, her hair, and blew out the candle flames, one by one.

The linen-wrapped hay quivered, just a moment, before the wind stole it into the abyss below.

Her offering—had Weles accepted it?

She gasped. "Weles, I thank You for hearing my prayer and for accepting my offering. I ask that You grant a whole fate, a green fate, seeded and good, to take the place of a broken one."

She just hoped that the intention would be enough. Her head bowed, she recited it three times, and then cleared the altar. By the time she was done, the darkness had started to creep in and with it a biting cold.

Snow fell in thick flakes onto her face. She breathed in the voices of the wood, those of the trees and plants and spirits, and weakened by the winter as they were, their scent swept a chilling finger up her spine, rattled her with a shiver. A feeling of foreboding settled in with it, moments before a mournful howl filled the air.

She peered among the trees. Nothing there but her own tracks in the snow.

Then the howl neared, its volume rattling her ribcage.

She reached for her vial of lake water.

Ravens perched in the willow trees, two, four, ten—twenty. And when they opened their beaks, they yowled like cats.

A woman screamed, ear splitting and blood curdling.

Brygida rushed toward the sound, ready to summon the wrath of the blood. Had a villager wandered into the forest on her own?

Among the snow-battered tree trunks, a woman cowered, her back to Brygida. And behind her—

Behind her—

Blazing red eyes glowed beneath a set of curled black horns. Shadows dripped from the sharp quills of dark fur, jutting out from a massive form as big as the surrounding oaks. Branches groaned and broke to accommodate its form.

Its jaws snapped at the woman, who raised her arm to shield herself from it.

Drawing upon the wrath of the blood, Brygida called the snow from the oaks, the banks upon the land. White powder turned glacial, forged into spears of ice barraging toward the demon.

Whispers seeped into her mind like fingers, stroking and scratching, sifting through her thoughts as the ice paused just short of the demon.

Brygida doubled over, clutching at her head. *Get out, get out!*

The woman whimpered and fled, but she tripped, falling face first into the snow. As she scrambled, her hood fell back. White-blond hair. Lady Rubin?

The fingers plunged deeper into Brygida's mind, sinking in like claws. Red eyes bored into hers, embedded in shadow like embers in ash.

Snow was only crystallized water. And she was a water witch.

Clutching her vial of lake water so hard it might shatter, she kicked off her boots, plunging her bare feet into the frigid snow.

With a primal scream, she transformed every flake of snow into ice spears that plunged straight toward the demon. It lunged for her, icicles impaling its thigh as it raked its claws across her hand.

She stumbled back, wrapping her bleeding wound

in her cloak. The demon crept closer in the silence—Lady Rubin had stopped screaming.

Brygida scrambled away from the demon's maw, its hot breath fanning on her face.

It reared back, roaring.

Someone grabbed her by the arm, yanking her onto horseback. They raced through the forest.

"Are you all right?" asked Halina, glancing back toward the demon. They leaped over fallen trees swallowed up by snow, and weaved through the oaks and pines, brushing against their branches and scattering the snow from them.

"There's a woman back there!" Brygida shouted over the wind. "We can't leave her!"

Halina shook her head. "It's too late for her. She's been bitten by the *bies*."

Brygida struggled against her, but Halina was stronger and broader. Over her shoulder, the wind picked up and snow flurries fell down around her, obscuring her view. "I serve Mokosza. I can't just leave her!"

Halina shook her head. "There's serving Mokosza, and there's just being foolish. We can't save her without risking your life and mine."

"Then let me go! I decide what's worth risking my life for."

"Not going to happen, *maleńka*."

Oh yes it would.

With a swift backward jab, Brygida caught Halina in the gut, and her grip loosened.

Brygida fell from the saddle, landing hard in the snow but just shy of the horse's hooves, praise Mokosza.

After a moment of shock, she struggled to her feet, the snow melting to lukewarm water where her bare soles touched the earth. She ran as fast as she could back to where she'd last seen the bies.

But when she returned, there was nothing.

Nothing but her boots, drops of blood in the snow... and the bies's tracks, leading away.

❦

Clouds of vapor escaped Kaspian's chapped lips with each exhalation. Running away was what he was best at, and today was no different. The snow had melted and refrozen, and he had to stab the legs of his easel through the crust of ice to stabilize it.

In this weather, he'd have to work quickly. Ashen clouds gathered on the horizon, threatening snowfall. The dull light stripped the landscape of any variance and left it as a drab blob. This wasn't an ideal time to sketch, let alone be away from a warm fire. But when he was at his most restless, art was the only balm.

He'd tried painting in his room, but each time he'd brought brush to canvas, the rattle of Tata's cough or the murmur of voices coming in and out of Mama and

Tata's chambers had diluted his focus. And instead of forgetting just for a little while, his thoughts would circle one another. One week. Mama's silence. The crushing weight of his responsibility. Each thought chased the other, like a dog running circles in a kennel. If his thoughts spun even a minute more, he would go mad.

Out here in the stillness and quiet of winter, his thoughts stilled. The charcoal became an extension, from which he could pour out all his emotions. There wasn't much time to work—with Tata ill, his responsibilities had fallen to Kaspian. His fingers fumbled with the charcoal in his gloves, and it was difficult to get the right grip.

You are truly an ungrateful child, Mama had said. The sharp barbs they'd flung at one another became thick lines on canvas.

Did she really find his judgment so lacking that he'd bring someone into their home to harm Tata? And what about her interlude with Lord Granat? What had that been? A diplomatic ploy, or... or something else? For his entire life, he'd believed his parents' marriage was perfect. But too many of his beliefs had turned out to be lies as of late.

He clenched the charcoal and broke it in half, then discarded it and retrieved another. When it met the canvas, this time the strokes were long and languorous, like a slow-moving stream. One week. Two, if the gods were kind. That was all Tata had to left to live. Little by little, black covered the white canvas, only a dark smudge left on his glove as he finished and let his hand fall to his side.

Like the charcoal, Tata's life was running out. Wouldn't this time be better spent together, instead of working out the spinning thoughts inside? Had he known Roksana's time was limited, would he have run away like this? Closing off his head and heart to avoid the truth? Or would he have tried to catch every last moment with her before it was too late...?

Over and over he'd returned here. To this spot, attempting to capture it. The place he'd last seen Roksana. But no matter how many attempts he made, he couldn't immortalize this place, that moment he'd let her go. In today's attempt, the black smeared, the lines lacked definition and turned to a muddled gray. The tree he'd tried to draw was crooked and twisted, devoid of life.

With a heavy sigh, he ran a hand over his face. He needed a drink. His head throbbed from last night's indulgence, and the only cure for it seemed to be drinking more.

"Are you sketching in this weather?" a familiar voice asked.

He glanced back. Beneath a heavy woolen cloak and a pink scarf covering the bottom half of her face, Nina was nearly unrecognizable. A strand of her blond hair peeked out from beneath her hood and fell onto her rosy cheeks. What was she doing here?

He'd been so absorbed in his own thoughts he hadn't even heard her approach. The wind picked up and pierced through the layers of wool he wore. Most people were locked inside during these short, frigid winter days; it was strange for her to be out and about.

With his back to his sketch, he blocked the atrocity from her view. He hated for anyone to see a work in progress, much less such a failure as this one.

"Was there something I could help you with?" he asked, quirking an eyebrow. Most of the village hardly gave him the time of day anymore, and Nina, who'd once given evidence against him, should want nothing to do with him.

Unless... was this a setup? Were the peasants who'd spread the rumors about him planning on attacking him? Were they here, waiting to spring a trap? His mind retreated back to the feel of innumerable hands holding him in place, his blade far from his grip, and the glint of a knife raised, ready to cut into his flesh...

Heart at the back of his throat, he jerked his head around to survey the landscape. At the edge of a snow-covered field, Dariusz stood menacingly behind a stone fence, nearly one with a post. But apart from them, there was no one else around, only the sound of the wind over stark fields, and a few stripped trees lining the muddy and icy road.

"I just saw you out here and thought I'd say hello." She cleared her throat as she turned her head back toward the family farm. Her scarf slipped, and he caught a glimpse of her split lip.

No doubt her father's doing. A man who'd raise a hand to his wife wouldn't exempt his child. And if Dariusz stood there watching, perhaps this meeting was his doing, too. Still angling to marry off his daughter?

As much as he wanted to resent Nina for thinking him capable of murder, he pitied her more than anything. The man she'd loved had lied to her, had been a monster the witches had dealt with. Her father, on the other hand, was a monster *not* yet dealt with.

If he chased her away, Dariusz was likely to take it out on her. In these cold winter months, there was little to do aside from sitting by the hearth and drinking. And everyone knew Dariusz beat his wife, Zofia, when he was drunk, and now it seemed he had moved on to Nina as well.

Although Tata had never said it aloud to him, he'd looked the other way and ignored Zofia's plight while Dariusz had continued to provide him with coin.

That wasn't how the Wolski family would do things. Not anymore. He couldn't save both Zofia and Nina by dealing with Dariusz yet, but perhaps he could take Nina out of there.

"If you ever wanted to leave home, there's a safe

place for you at the manor. A job, if you want." It was the least he could offer.

Nina shrank down into her scarf, pulling it up over her nose. "My mother needs me on the farm, but thank you for the offer."

Of course... she didn't want to leave her mother to deal with Dariusz alone. If he had the power right now, he'd see Dariusz pay for his treatment of his wife and daughter. And once he was lord, he would see that Dariusz did pay.

But in the meantime, Dariusz had sent his daughter here for a reason, one that came with the risk of physical harm if she failed.

Nina stood in the quiet. Would something small appease her father? Some indication that Nina could be the next Lady Rubin?

"I was planning on heading back to the manor. May I walk you home?"

"Oh." She blushed, but her downward gaze wasn't flirtatious. Her shoulders curved inward, and her eyes faded. She was ashamed. "You don't have to..."

"I don't want you to get in trouble," he said with a half-smile he hoped was comforting.

She nodded slowly, hiding her face. They walked side by side, snow crunching beneath their boots, as a few snowflakes began to fall. At the Baran fence, they turned a corner and lost sight of Dariusz. He felt as if he should say something to break the awkward silence, but what was there to say to a woman whose testimony had almost gotten him killed?

He cleared his throat. "It's been rather cold." The weather. Always safe to discuss that.

"It has."

They lapsed into silence once more. This was nothing like the comfortable silences he shared with Brygida. They could walk side by side for hours with hardly a word shared between them, and it felt as if they'd bared their souls to one another.

What was Brygida doing now? If only she'd show up to rescue him from this awkward encounter. A hex or two for Dariusz wouldn't be unwelcome either.

When the snow started to fall in earnest, they turned back toward her farm. As they approached the gates, a gust of wind blew and pushed back Nina's hood, exposing her dark-blond plait.

Roksana.

Nina's hair was more of a burnished gold than a true gold like Roksana's, for just a split second it was almost as if she were alive again. There had been countless times he'd walked Roksana home in this same way; the Baran and Malicki lands bordered one another. But Nina wasn't Roksana.

She pulled up her hood once more and dipped her head in thanks before heading through the gate. She took a few steps before turning to face him. "Why are you being kind to me? You could have sent me away, and it would have been within your right to do so. I'm sure Brygida told you what I thought I saw that night..."

He rubbed the back of his neck with a gloved hand. "You remind me a bit of... her. " Although he'd never been as close with Nina as he had been with Roksana, they were neighbors and had played together as children. There was a history there, albeit strained. "And you should know that if you're ever in need of help, you will always find it at the manor. I'll make sure of that."

She lowered her chin for a moment before clenching her hands. Her head shot up. "My father has been talking with Lord Granat. They've been exchanging letters for months. I thought you should know."

With a quick turn of her heel, she spun away and up the road back toward her hut.

Kaspian stood frozen in place. She'd caught him off guard, and by the time he had processed what she'd said, she'd disappeared.

Did this mean Dariusz was Lord Granat's spy? Had he been the one to report Tata's failing health?

If Dariusz had allied with Lord Granat, he could turn the village against the entire Wolski family. And with Tata weakened and the village set against his alleged rapist-murderer heir, this could be the perfect chance to take all of Rubin.

But what if it was a bluff? Dariusz had sent Nina to

him after all... Was this his way of forcing them into a marriage? Was Dariusz really that cunning?

The snow fell heavier, and the wind picked up. A blizzard was brewing. He needed to get back home.

Mama would know what to do about Dariusz. No one could read people better than she could. But getting her advice meant breaking the silence that had stretched between them since their fight.

They'd both said hurtful things, especially him. He wasn't proud of how he'd acted, but it was clear he couldn't do this alone. It was time he stopped running away and faced his destiny.

He ran back to the manor, the frigid air burning his lungs. Snow crunched under his feet, and the wind blew harder, stronger, obscuring his vision until everything around him was just a blur of white and gray.

After racing up the oaken steps leading into the manor, he threw open the doors. The cold wind entered with him, and snow powdered the floor. People packed the main hall, and it thrummed with activity.

Stefan stood in the entryway, a frown marring his brow as he scanned the crowd. His hair stood at all angles, and he hadn't bothered to scrape the mud off his work boots, which was unlike him.

"Stefan," he called out, and Stefan met his gaze with an uncharacteristically somber expression.

His stomach dropped. No, it couldn't be. Ewa had

said Tata would hold on for at least another week or two.

"Is it my father? Is he all right?" His entire body ran cold. He hadn't even gotten the chance to say goodbye—

Stefan approached and put his hand on Kaspian's shoulder. "No, Lord Rubin is sleeping at the moment. His condition is unchanged. But..."

Kaspian exhaled, his shoulders falling with relief. If Tata was still breathing, then anything else Stefan said couldn't be nearly as bad. "Then what is it?"

"It's Lady Rubin. She... she's gone missing."

CHAPTER 7

The wind howled, shaking the roof, and shadows danced along the walls as the fire in the main hall's stone hearth wavered. Kaspian paced between oaken tables. Iskra, Mama's dog, followed at his heels. If it weren't for her normally placid dog's distressed whining, he would have thought this was all nothing.

What had driven Mama to leave the manor in this weather? Was it because they'd fought? He'd racked his mind trying to remember when he'd last seen her. Not since their fight. And after questioning all of the servants, none had seen her since then either. Was she out there somewhere caught in the storm, alone and afraid?

He dragged his hands through his hair. How could he stand here and do nothing when he should be out there looking for her, storm be damned? Servants and peasants gathered in the hall, grasped their tankards, and watched him pass by with hooded gazes, their whispers a mix of soft concern and muttered rumors.

As he approached, Stefan blocked his way, throwing his arms out.

"I'm not going to let you go out there and freeze to death," Stefan said, with an authoritative tone he rarely used on people. Although he'd used it to great effect on stubborn horses.

Kaspian balled his hand into a fist. "My mother is out there! I can't just stand by while she's in danger."

"This is Lady Rubin—she's no helpless maid. It's likely she's at a nearby farm waiting for the storm to pass, just like us." He gestured to the peasants and servants waiting in the hall. When a blizzard came, there was nothing to do but wait. Still, Tata was on his deathbed and Mama was missing, who knew where out in the blizzard. As acting lord, he should do something more than just have hot tea and blankets distributed to the waiting crowd.

He clenched his teeth so hard his jaw ached. Stefan would wrestle him to the ground if he attempted to pass. And considering how Stefan could control a horse that weighed five times as much as he did, just fighting him would take longer than the storm would take to pass. There was no choice but to wait.

Striding to the end of the hall, he aimed for the

head table, where just days before, Mama, Tata, and he had all shared a meal. That couldn't be the last time they'd ever be together.

A decanter of wine had been left out, and he filled a goblet, drained it in one gulp, and then poured a second, and a third. As he raised the third drink to his lips, Stefan put a hand over the rim.

"Slow down there."

Wine spilled over the top of his goblet as he pulled it away from Stefan.

"I just need to take the edge off my nerves." Kaspian gulped it greedily, before Stefan could wrest it from him.

Stefan frowned. It had become a more regular occurrence as of late. There was less teasing in his admonishments and more disapproving glances, but the last thing he needed now was his best friend's judgment.

At his feet, Iskra whimpered pitifully. He scratched behind her ears, trying to soothe her, but she continued to fidget beneath his touch, gleaming dark eyes trained on the door.

Stefan crossed his arms over his chest. "I'm worried about you. You haven't been yourself lately."

There was no disputing that statement. Who was he? He wasn't entirely sure anymore. Was he the rich heir who'd appeared to get away with murder? Or was he the daydreaming painter he'd been with Brygida?

Was he the struggling future lord of Rubin, who'd try his best for his people and yet never fully atone for an entire family's worth of transgressions?

After draining his fourth goblet, he set it down on the table and sank into a chair. He would have finished the entire decanter but for Stefan's nagging. Even though he'd only had four drinks, a pleasant warmth had already started to spread, dulling the edge of his nerves. His chin dropped to his chest.

"What if something awful happened to her, just like Roksana?" The wine had loosened his lips. He hated exposing this side of himself to anyone, but this entire scenario was too close to the Feast of Mokosza. If he had chased Roksana that night, he could have saved her, he just knew it. And leaving Mama alone in the cold... he might be damning her to a similar fate.

Stefan grasped both his shoulders and squeezed. "Don't think like that. Your mother is a battle-axe and can take care of herself. We'll bring her home, trust me."

With a ragged breath, he nodded, if only to appease Stefan. If something happened to Mama, he would never forgive himself. He wouldn't lose Tata and Mama, not fresh on the heels of losing Roksana. What had he done to offend the gods? Who would they take next? Stefan...? Brygida? Was everyone he loved doomed?

"Besides, no one, not even you, could find anything in this storm. There's no chance whatsoever you'll find your own hand in front of your face, let alone Lady Rubin," Stefan added. "And once it's over, do you think she wants to return home to find you frozen outside the front door like an icicle?"

He grimaced, but Stefan was right. As much as he wanted to do something, there was nothing to do right now but wait.

The storm raged outside, rattling shutters and howling like a pack of wolves. As soon as it passed, he would find her. No matter what.

❦

THE BACK OF BRYGIDA'S HAND THROBBED. THE SCRATCH the bies had left on her was red and inflamed. Mamusia waved incense of nettle leaf, white sage, coltsfoot, and horehound, and although it was thick, its potency would help remove any lingering traces of the bies's magic. The whole cottage filled with the smoky haze, a blurry film dulling the fire in the hearth.

Mama scowled at the scratch as she treated the wound, applying an unguent of witch hazel, vervain, cinquefoil, and blessed thistle, as well as some of Mamusia's stock of agrimony, which she used beneath her pillow for restful sleep when the Sight became too aggressive, but was also known for its healing properties. "What were you thinking? You could have been killed."

She would still be out there searching for Lady Rubin if the blizzard hadn't forced her to return home and seek shelter. And once the blizzard passed, she'd be back out there and wouldn't relent until she found Lady Rubin. She wasn't about to give up on a demon's victim, let alone Kaspian's mother.

Halina leaned against the far wall, hands on her hips. "This isn't normal behavior for a bies, out in the daylight in the middle of protected witchlands. This seems like the fury of Weles." She shook her head, with a suspicious glance toward Brygida.

Had Halina seen her make the offering?

Mama pressed a cloth with herbs to the scratch, and it burned. Brygida yanked her hand back. The mark had changed colors from red to a deep black, like ash. That... wasn't something she'd seen before.

Mama's eyes grew wide. "This isn't just a scratch. You've been blackmarked." Mama took a deep breath, but a tremble wove through her. "Something did happen on Kolęda. I never should have let you go—"

"Ewa, let's not overreact," Mamusia cautioned.

Mama's livid gaze snapped to Mamusia's. "How can I not? This isn't just a scratch, Liliana. This is serious!"

Brygida swallowed past a lump in her throat. "What does it mean to be blackmarked?"

Halina and Mama shared a look. She didn't like what it said. Not one bit. Her stomach squirmed.

"Ewa?" Mamusia prompted, her voice trembling.

"The Huntresses of Dziewanna... You've dealt with *biesy* before, haven't you?"

Mama rose and reached for a book on the shelf, her Wilk grimoire. It held all her notes on treating patients, as well as her line's wisdom and spells, just like the Mrok grimoire. She flipped the pages and set it on the table in front of Brygida. "Is this the demon you saw?"

She stared down at the rendering of the creature— Halina had called it a bies. Red eyes, horns, sharp spikes of fur clad in shadow. It was exactly what she'd seen. Her throat tightened. "It is."

Mama blinked over her vivid green eyes, and they watered, welling with unshed tears. "The... the black-mark will expand and grow, claiming your arm and poisoning your mind... until it reaches your heart," she said, her voice breaking. "And it will... kill you."

A chill rattled her spine. Kill? Mama did not use that word lightly. Her heart beat faster, but she swallowed and took a deep breath, willing it to slow.

The broken piece of hay. Had it been... had it been a true death omen after all?

And Lady Rubin, who'd refused her hospitality...? Had they both fallen to Weles's fury?

But this couldn't be the end. She was still here. As long as her heart kept beating, her lungs kept breathing, the fight wasn't over. She wouldn't give up on herself, nor Lady Rubin.

"How do I stop it?" Brygida asked, unable to keep the tremble from her voice.

"There's only one way," Halina said with a grim look in her eye. "Catch and kill the bies."

Mamusia stood by the window, her shawl wrapped tightly around her, and covered her mouth. Tears rolled down her cheeks.

"Can you help her?" Mama asked Halina.

"If Weles has sent this bies in response to an offering, it is the supplicant who must slay it." Halina locked eyes with her. There was a hunger there, and perhaps more, a narrowed envy. Mama had told her stories about the honor of the huntresses; a kill brought prestige, and by being blackmarked, she had taken that chance from Halina. "But yes, I can help. Biesy can control minds, so I might be able to keep it distracted." The huntresses' coven was immune to demons' powers, a gift from Holy Dziewanna.

"Brygida... what did you ask of Weles?" Mama asked, her chin quivering. She rubbed it with a firm hand.

That would mean sharing what had happened at the manor. It could mean never being allowed to see Kaspian ever again. "I—I—"

"The truth. Now!" Mama demanded, grabbing her arm.

Brygida squeezed her eyes shut. Two lives hung in the balance. "I drew a broken piece of hay during the telling of my fate. I offered it to Weles and asked for Him to change it."

Tears streamed down Mama's reddening face. "You foolish child, you think the Horned Serpent changes fates out of the goodness of His heart?" Mama shook her shoulders. "He's sent you a challenge. The challenge of a god, do you understand?"

She shivered. The challenge of a god...? Weles would deign to do such a thing?

"A challenge means it can be defeated," Mamusia's thin voice interrupted from the window.

Mama shook her head and waved her off angrily. So Mama believed it hopeless, then.

Defeat Weles's challenge... defeat the bies... Was that even possible? Her attempts to use the wrath of the blood against it had been ineffectual. "I... I'm not sure. It entered my mind, controlled my blood. Alone, I'm not sure I can... I..."

"The storm has passed, but I fear a greater one awaits," Mamusia said, her voice distant. It was the voice of prophecy, and the hairs on her arms stood on end.

"We better get on the move now and start tracking it before it gets too far," Halina said, grasping her bow.

Mama's expression was grim, and Mamusia still looked far away, her gaze half dreaming. Brygida steeled herself; even if it was hopeless, she wouldn't wait here for the blackmark to claim her heart. There was nothing to do but face the challenge.

"You'll need that." Halina nodded toward the Scythe of the Mother.

It had been a long time since her hand had held the wisdom of generations. She hadn't touched it since the rusałki had been appeased.

She approached the altar reverently, hands trembling. As soon as it was in her grasp, the power flowed through her, the voices of the Mrok witches before her whispering.

"Mama..." she said with a tenuous half-smile. "Can I leave the cottage?"

With a sad laugh, Mama wiped at her face, sniffing as she gathered her composure, running trembling fingers over her thick dark-red braid. "Yes, my child. I fear you must, and straight into danger's waiting embrace." Mama held out the rabbit-fur cloak while Mamusia filled a pack. Then they both already knew her choice, and they supported her in it.

"I'll fight it, with everything Mokosza has granted me and everything you've both taught me, and I'll come home." She let a tearful Mama cloak her and accepted the pack from Mamusia.

"By Her thread, Brygida," Mamusia said, and Mama echoed the words, crossing her arms tightly.

Brygida bowed her head, silently praying she'd see both their faces again. "By Her thread."

They threw their arms around her, whispering words of comfort, and if she listened to them too long, she'd want to stay here forever, lose her nerve. Biting back tears, she pulled away.

With a last look back, she followed Halina out of the cottage, and got into the saddle behind her.

"Do you feel it?" Halina asked her, unnaturally still, attentive.

Brygida stared at her. "Feel what?"

Halina shook her head and tsked. "The invader on your witchlands. That's why we needed the scythe." She rolled her eyes. "It will give us a trail here. No huntress takes spoor for granted."

Brygida closed her eyes and concentrated, listening to the sound of the wind through the trees, the slow plop of snow from overburdened branches, and beneath it all... an angry whisper, a hiss and agitation, the forest's voice warning her, guiding her.

"It's this way." She pointed with the scythe, and they followed the hiss through the woods, struggled through large embankments of snow.

The farther they traveled, the stronger the feeling became, the more it made her skin twitch and crawl.

Then she found the drops of blood in the snow... alongside footprints leading up to a body.

CHAPTER 8

K aspian woke with a crick in his neck and bright white light illuminating the hall. The household served breakfast to the scattered villagers remaining.

The storm had finally passed, and morning had come.

Several things happened quickly. A search party gathered, a mixed group of servants, villagers, and guards, led by the captain, Rafał. Stefan and the other stable hands saddled horses for the guards and Kaspian.

Stefan held onto Demon's reins as he entered the yard, his sword belted at his waist. The black gelding stomped his foot impatiently as Kaspian swung into the saddle, while Iskra yelped and bolted for the closed manor gates, clearly refusing to be excluded.

Under the captain's command, they broke apart into groups, to better cover ground in the fastest time possible. Kaspian rode with his entourage, his heart in his throat.

Just let her be safe.

Mama had to be fine. It was likely as Stefan had said: she'd taken shelter in a local farmhouse. They'd find her and bring her home, and everything would go back to how it had been. He would apologize for his harsh words, and they would find strength and comfort one another through Tata's final days on this earth.

One by one, they checked barns, farmhouses, and sheds, only to come up empty handed. The blizzard had covered the landscape in large embankments of snow, burying stone walls and partially obscuring solitary farmhouses.

If Mama had gotten caught out in the storm, she might have frozen to death... If that had happened, they wouldn't find her body until spring.

Shuddering, he clenched the reins tighter, and Demon danced beneath him, skirting off the road into an embankment up to his hocks. And as Iskra sniffed at each one, her white fur disappeared, the matching pale snowbanks swallowing her up. She trudged forward, making a trench in the snow, her tail low and her ears back. If she didn't react, then there was hope they wouldn't discover Mama's body.

Mokosza, protector of women, please let her be safe. I beg of You.

Their search led them farther and farther from the manor. With dead ends at every turn, Kaspian's shoulders slumped. Why had he fought with her? She had only been trying to do what she'd thought was best. He should have been more patient, more understanding, placed his love and respect for her above his anger—

Iskra barked, and his stomach dropped. Had Iskra found her? Alive. Alive. She had to be alive.

Demon huffed, twin clouds of breath drifting up from his nostrils.

Kaspian surveyed the horizon. Sunlight reflected off the snow banks, and he had to shade his eyes. Wind whistled across the dark woods, and the branches on the trees creaked and groaned. But despite the blinding light overhead, shadows seemed to linger around the trees. The hairs stood on the back of his neck as he gripped the reins tightly.

When he'd wandered the crooked pathways through the woods with Brygida, it had been a welcoming and enchanting place. Now he was only left with a feeling of foreboding. If only Brygida were here, she could find Mama with her lake water. But he couldn't involve her in his troubles anymore. He'd put her in enough danger as it was.

Iskra barked louder and bolted for the woods.

One of the guards followed after her, and so did Kaspian.

His heart thumped in his ears.

"Over here! We've found something," the guard shouted.

Kaspian dug his heels into Demon's side. The gelding reared and bolted forward in a burst of speed, kicking up freshly fallen snow. It had grayed where the guards had trodden, leading up to a small embankment.

There, a guard stood next to his mount, his gaze on the ground just out of sight. The other members of his search party joined them and stood in a half circle.

"This must be the witches' doing," a guard said as they all approached.

"They've cursed this village. You saw how she sabotaged the offering," a second guard murmured.

"Don't be fools. What did you find?" Kaspian asked as he swung down from the saddle.

The guard straightened and moved back, revealing flecks of crimson upon the snow. Blood.

His throat clenched.

A trail of blood led away, disappearing over a snowbank and further obscured by a fallen tree. Its branches grasped outward like claws, hungry and waiting.

Something had carved deep gashes into the bark, and its stump was nothing but jagged fragments bleeding sap. Large indentations had crushed the snow around it and followed the trail of blood into the forest.

Footprints. Twice as big as a man's, almost wolf like, but bigger than any wolf he'd ever seen. And powerful enough to fell a tree?

"This is a bad omen. The witches took Lady Rubin," Rafał said with a shake of his head, then stroked his pale beard ruminatively.

A few rapid blinks to clear his vision, but the blood was still there, like paint splashed on a canvas.

"No," he said. "This is something else. The witches can't harm women, remember?" He didn't know what yet, but it couldn't be Brygida or her mothers' doing. They would never do something like this. No matter how the village scorned them, they weren't murderers.

Gray clouds rolled in, casting long shadows over their party. He couldn't explain the blood and the monstrous footprint. He'd seen things in the forest, heard stories of demons. Brygida had assured him that the witches' protection kept the village safe.

But the offering she'd drawn... and how Mama had thrown her out... Could this be Weles's fury?

His hands shook as he glanced around, eyes skimming over frost-covered ferns and patches of earth breaking with thin crusts of ice, where the snow had melted and refrozen.

The blood had to be wolves hunting a deer. It wasn't Mama. One of the other search parties had likely already found her, and she was safe at the manor. But he had to confirm it was a deer with his own eyes. "I'm going to investigate."

"The woods are dangerous," Rafał said.

Holding his gaze, Kaspian drew his sword. "So are we."

Ignoring the guards' protests, he trudged through the snow bank, careful not to disturb the bloody trail. As he got closer, the blood trail grew thicker, melting the snow in places, and he could no longer see the guards through the copse of trees. A restless wind drifted through the forest, a cold touch brushing against his neck.

Lying on the ground was a cloaked body, golden blond hair stained with blood, splayed out in the blood-soaked snow.

"Perun's bright lightning," he bit out under his breath, rushing to the person. It couldn't be Mama. This couldn't be happening again.

"Kaspian?" Brygida's gentle voice.

He lifted his gaze as if in a dream. Brygida's eyes, sorrowful violet eyes, fixed upon the person's body. A few feet behind her, a woman with auburn hair drew her bow and pointed it at him.

He held up his hands.

"I don't mean you any harm." His eyes flicked from the body to the strange woman.

"He's a friend." Brygida stood between Kaspian and the woman.

The woman did not lower her weapon but kept it trained on him. His gaze was torn between the threat and the body lying on the ground.

Brygida knelt in the snow beside the victim, then turned the person over.

A man.

It wasn't Mama.

Kaspian collapsed to his knees in the snow.

It wasn't her. Praise the gods, it wasn't her.

"Enemies," the woman gritted out to Brygida, and nodded toward the trees behind him.

The guards and peasants filtered in through the maze of trunks.

"Capture them!" Rafał shouted, pointing with his sword. "Defend Master Kaspian!"

As the guards rushed forward, Kaspian sprang to his feet instantly. Brygida stood, reaching for her vial of lake water, the tips of her fingers stained black down past her knuckles.

"Don't touch her!" Kaspian shouted, placing himself between her and the guards, his sword leveled at them.

The guards, Brygida, and the other woman stood in a silent standoff. Brygida clutched her vial, and the woman aimed her arrow at Rafał.

"I told you the witches were behind this, and look,

here they are," Rafał said, pointing his blade at Brygida and the woman.

"They found him just as we did," Kaspian replied. Then to Brygida, he said, "Get out of here," and jerked his head toward the forest.

She hesitated for just a moment before bolting back into the concealment of the trees. The other woman lingered behind, her arrow trained on them before she too fled after Brygida. The guards stood around him, faces grim.

"You'd let those murderers escape?" Rafał closed in, halting at the tip of his sword. "That's Paweł, the cooper's son!"

"She did nothing wrong." He didn't retract his blade even a hair's breadth.

"Can you say that when she was standing over the corpse?"

"This obviously wasn't done by human hands. Look." Kaspian gestured to the mangled body. An arm had nearly been pulled from the socket, hanging on by only the merest strip of flesh. Deep gashes covered his chest and body, as if clawed. A human couldn't have done this. Only a demon.

"Witches can turn into demons," a guard said, his eyes tracing the footprints leading deeper into the forest, where Brygida had escaped.

"No, they can't." Kaspian locked in a stare with Rafał.

"You are the future lord of Rubin," Rafał said slowly. "It would be wise to remember who your allies are."

"I haven't forgotten," he said darkly. But it was they who had forgotten their place. "Now have this body taken to the manor and continue the search for Lady Rubin. I order you not to engage the witches. Report any findings to me at once."

Rafał held his gaze for a moment longer before he nodded. "Yes, my lord." All the guards sheathed their blades and stirred to action.

Kaspian, too, sheathed his sword, but the threat was far from over. Today Rafał had decided not to challenge him further. Today. But the next time could turn out differently, and as he passed the blood drops in the snow, he was only too keenly aware.

But he'd worry about that tomorrow. Today, he still had to find Mama. Alive.

CHAPTER 9

A fter running into Kaspian and the villagers, Brygida continued the hunt with Halina, but every thicket evoked those contorted faces, every tangle of bare branches the lines of hatred and vitriol. She and her mothers had never been welcome, but to be so openly despised and threatened? Kaspian had been forced to level a sword at his own guards. Although his defense of her warmed her heart, it was a dire state of affairs that he'd had to.

Whatever had turned the tide against them so swiftly in the village, she'd have to discuss it with Kaspian and find a way to remedy it; but right now, they both had more pressing concerns.

In less than a day, the blackmark had spread to cover the entire back of her hand. Left unchecked, it would spread and kill her.

And despite nearly a full day of searching, she'd found no hint of Lady Rubin. It was as if she'd disappeared altogether. When Kaspian had found that poor man killed, he'd looked shaken to the bone... If only she could have given him some solace, some answers. But as it was, she feared telling him what she'd already seen.

The forest's agitation had grown so fierce that it made her head ache. Apparitions screaming in the woods, haunting their steps, and the very trees battling one another with their stark limbs. The beast that had hunted on these sacred witchlands and a victim's blood staining the snow... it had made the forest more restless than usual.

A haze shrouded her vision, not unlike the deep exhaustion that claimed her some nights, but she couldn't blink it away. She leaned against an oak, its rough bark brushing her forehead, her head pounding as she tried to shut out the voices in her head.

"It's gone beyond your witchlands now," Halina said, kneeling in the snow next to the frozen carcass of a deer, the innards missing along with nearly the entire back half.

"What now?" Brygida asked, using the scythe to stand up straighter. It couldn't be too late. There had to be something she could do yet.

"If you want to live, we continue our hunt." Halina's eyes sparkled, something predatory stirring there, and she stared past the edge of the forest, into the wilds. "Beyond your witchlands."

Beyond her witchlands? She'd hardly stepped outside them into the village, but to leave her home behind was unfathomable. "I need to talk to my mothers first. I can't just leave without a word."

"This won't stop." Halina tapped the back of Brygida's hand. "That blackmark will continue to grow and corrupt your mind before it claims your life. You're wasting time, if you want to live."

At the cottage, telling her mothers she'd have to leave their witchlands would upset them, but in the end, they'd agree she had to do it, if it meant treating her blackmark. As much as she wanted to tell them she was leaving, Halina was right. "What about Lady Rubin? What happened to her?"

"Dead, most likely." Halina shrugged.

Such a casual dismissal of human life. She couldn't understand it. "But what if she isn't? Couldn't the bies have taken her?"

"It's possible, if she was his target."

The night of Kolęda, she'd drawn broken hay, yes. But in doing so, she'd also moved Lady Rubin to rescinding her hospitality. Their fates were tied, and if Weles had sent the bies to challenge her, perhaps Lady Rubin had also been challenged. There was hope she was still alive.

Did Halina not wish to consult her grimoire, or did she not have one? She'd known something about demons, but Mama had kept copious notes in hers. Halina rubbed her hands together, brushing snow from her gloves with a blank stare. Halina truly didn't care about Lady Rubin's fate whatsoever.

But Brygida pushed on. "Where would he have taken her?"

"That I cannot say for certain."

Her hand was black as night, and she was running out of time, yes. But her greatest strength had always been with her family. She chewed her lip hard enough that she tasted blood. Mama had notes on the bies and Mamusia could See. Maybe with both their strengths, she could find the bies *and* Lady Rubin. "I know who can. My mothers."

Halina raised a dark eyebrow. "Wasting time to go back?"

"Either that, or wasting time to search without a lead," Brygida replied. "At least if we return, we might have notes from Mama or a vision from Mamusia, either of which could point us in the right direction. 'No huntress takes spoor for granted, isn't that right?"

With a wolf-like grin, Halina nodded. "Aye, maleńka. You're not wrong."

With that, they mounted up and headed back to the cottage. The thought of returning home to her mothers' smiling faces, only to have to tell them she'd failed and would have to leave their witchlands, made her heart sink. But there was nothing for it. Besides, this was what her mothers had always taught her: to never give up, and to use her head before using her magic.

Before long, the familiar resounding cracks and thuds greeted her before the sight of Mama chopping wood. They had plenty as it was, and the pile that would last them through the rest of next year had now grown to nearly Mama's height.

When Mama looked up, she dropped the duller axe into the snow and, her face bright, rushed forward to take Brygida's hand. As she turned it over, her expression fell.

Brygida shook her head.

Mamusia came to the door, her violet eyes glowing in the dying light of day. "I've seen you going on a journey through dangerous lands," she said in her dreaming voice.

"What about Lady Rubin, Mamusia? Did you see her?" Brygida prompted.

Mamusia shook her head. "No. Only darkness and a goodbye."

Brygida brushed her fingers over the blackmark. Was this what the hay had foretold? She refused to believe it. She would find the bies and kill it. She had to. "I—I have a feeling that the bies took Lady Rubin, but

I'm not sure how to find it. We haven't been able to pick up its trail again."

Mama's head drooped. "If you believe she was taken, I... I know how you might track it down."

"You do?" Brygida dismounted.

"I kept reading after you'd left, and... you'll need something of hers as a focus. If the bies truly has her, then scrying for her will help you find it," Mama added, then retreated into the cottage.

"Isn't that good news?" Halina asked, sliding out of the saddle and patting her horse. "Why is she so dour?"

With a sad smile, Mamusia approached and took Brygida's hand, squeezing it. "Oh, it's because Brygida will have to return to that young man's manor to retrieve something of his mother's."

The last thing Mama would ever want.

Halina leveled a sour look at Mamusia. "Are you sure it's wise to let your daughter among them?"

Mamusia's shoulders tensed as her gaze flickered toward the cottage, and Mama.

Halina held her palms up. "It's your decision to make. Either way, we'll leave at first light." Without another word, she led her horse away to tether it.

"Come." Mamusia's warm hand closed around hers as they headed into the cottage. As much as she wanted to see Kaspian, she didn't want to go to him bearing bad news, especially not after how the guards had behaved.

She could take care of herself, but her presence now would only cause him more trouble.

But what choice did she have? The curse was already spreading, and how many more people would the bies hurt unless it was stopped? It was on her for not sacrificing the hay in the first place, for resisting the omen.

If she hadn't, perhaps they wouldn't have incited Weles's fury... but the time for that choice had already passed. There was but one path before her now, and by the grace of the Mother, she would walk it and survive.

❧

AT THE FIRST LIGHT OF DAY, MAMA AND MAMUSIA waited to say goodbye to her. Overnight, the blackmark had covered her hands and spread up to her wrist, progressing quickly. Mamusia enveloped her into a fierce hug, and Mama grasped her from the other side.

"Stay safe, and come home to us," Mamusia said into her hair.

Brygida choked back the tears that threatened to spill down her cheeks. "I promise I will."

She hugged them harder, trying to imprint the feeling of comfort that was their embrace. But as she pulled away, she felt a cold wind's bite. There was a look in Mamusia's eyes that left her feeling uneasy, as if there was something more she wasn't telling her.

There was no clear line to mark the border between her witchlands and those beyond, at least not in sight, but when they'd been chasing the bies before, she'd felt it. Like an invisible barrier she should not cross. Had that been another witchlands? Or untended forest?

What she could do, what Halina could do, might not be enough to vanquish a single demon. And yet beyond their small quest lay a swallowing chaos that could consume endlessly, with nothing and no one strong enough to stop it.

They approached the Perun-struck oak, and soon they would be out of the familiarity of her witchlands and at the manor house, where she'd have to break the terrible news to Kaspian.

But it was better than it could have been, since if she was right, at least Lady Rubin was alive.

Halina urged her horse forward, onto the well-worn road leading toward the village. Given the guards' behavior, they'd likely be met with open hostility. She clutched the Scythe of the Mother closer. Hopefully without her regalia, there wouldn't be a panic about another murder. That poor young man had met a sad fate, and the villagers were rightfully angry, but she wasn't going to back down this time. Lady Rubin's fate, and her own, depended on her success.

The pressure that had been building in her started to ease some as the manor came into view. They'd gone unaccosted thus far. Perhaps the villagers had heeded common wisdom and kept indoors while the bies remained on the loose, but there would be no riding right into the courtyard. Not after they'd seen her beside the body of that village man.

She directed Halina around the back, where during the spring and summer, the horses had grazed. She slid off and sidled along the barn that abutted the fields, while Halina remained at a small distance, eyeing her dubiously.

Please let Stefan be here. Please. Doubtless any other stable hand would scream for dear life at the sight of her.

She knocked on the barn door. After holding her breath for several long seconds, it opened. A pointed pitchfork filled the doorway, and her heart pounded in her ears.

Stefan's bay-brown eyes widened, and he set aside the tool with a surprised smirk. "Now *you* were not who I was expecting to be knocking at my door today."

Had he been waiting for someone? Never mind.

"I have a favor to ask. I need to see Kaspian. It's important. And, well, I'm not exactly welcome by the guards right now."

Dusting off his hands, he gave her a lopsided smile, and with a bow and a flourish, he led her into the barn before closing the door behind him. "We're going to have to sneak you in. You're right—some of the village isn't very happy with you at the moment."

"I know, but I think I have a solution. And a way to find Lady Rubin."

"Well, that's quite the promise. Follow me, then." He waved for her to follow him, and they headed toward the manor together.

CHAPTER 10

Kaspian massaged his temples as Stryjek closed the door to Tata's office behind yet another villager. The demands that the witches pay for the death of the cooper's son had been piling up all day. With Mama still missing, rumors circulated that she'd been taken by the witches as well. The search continued, with guards spreading outward, to farther and farther corners of Rubin. He would be out there heading the search himself, if this never-ending stream of complaints would cease.

"May I give you some advice?" Stryjek stopped opposite Kaspian, with Tata's desk between them.

Perun's bright lightning, more than anything he needed advice. It felt wrong to be sitting here, in Tata's position. How many times had he stood in Stryjek's place, head bowed as Tata scolded him for mischief he'd gotten up to with Stefan? But although he was seated as a lord, with Stryjek standing over him, he still felt very much like the child in need of chastisement.

He leaned back in the chair and rubbed his brow. "It would be welcome. I am honestly out of my depth here."

"Give the people what they want." Stryjek turned his palms upward in a gesture of surrender. "Complaints resolved. Happy peasants. You get to live a while longer without a riot."

Kaspian sat up straight and frowned. Perhaps he'd misunderstood Stryjek's words. "Are you implying that I should blame Brygida for what was clearly a demon attack?"

Stryjek shrugged. "I've seen a lot in my travels. And what was done to that body could not have been done by one young woman, or even three women."

"But?" Kaspian prompted.

Growing up, he'd felt a certain comraderie to Stryjek, being that they were both second sons. If he was honest, he'd envied Stryjek's lifestyle, unfettered by duty, free to travel from region to region, only on occasion returning to Rubin with tales of his adventures and presents for him and Henryk.

He'd been a child when he'd last seen Stryjek. So perhaps he'd romanticized his recollections, making him more than he'd been, or maybe he was hoping for advice that Stryjek wasn't equipped to give.

"I think you've underestimated the power of fear, nephew. The people see what they want. And after Kolęda, they believe that a witch is capable of a whole lot more than what's possible. If you leave that specter to linger, every bout of bad weather and every lost farm animal will be the witches' fault, and if you keep taking their side, don't believe that being lord will save you, or this family. It won't."

Kaspian clenched the edge of the table, his fingernails scraping into the wood. "Brygida is my... friend."

Stryjek shrugged again. "You've got to look out for yourself and your family, too. And you can find another... 'friend.'"

It was easy for Stryjek to say that. He didn't know and love Brygida, see her goodness and that of her mothers, nor feel the collective breath the village had taken when Julian had been reaped for Roksana's murder. Not only did she and her mothers not deserve this, but they served an essential role in society that was now being attacked by rumors and factions. Once they were maneuvered out of the way by the powers manipulating all this, what new threat would await? And without the witches protecting them, would the people, his family, or this land survive?

Come the spring thaw, Stryjek would be gone, back on a new adventure. Perhaps not to return for years or ever again. Even if it weren't unthinkable to him and morally reprehensible, throwing the witches to the wolves would spare this family for only a breath but leave them vulnerable to a more dangerous predator.

Kaspian rubbed his forehead. Meanwhile, come spring, he would be left with disgruntled villagers... alone. The very prospect struck him cold. If that was the fate that awaited him anyway, he still would rather risk the village's ire on himself than make Brygida into a murderer. He drummed his fingers on the desktop, his gaze flickering to the door. Their anger could be a powerful force, one he was all too aware of.

But finding a scapegoat was not an option. And he had dire matters of life and death to handle right now with his parents, and no resources to uncover the source of the rumors. Nina had mentioned her father exchanging letters with Lord Granat, but surely they wouldn't risk throwing all of Rubin into upheaval, not when Lord Granat and Mama had planned a wedding for him and the Bear of Granat? Besides, Dariusz was a malcontent, but he didn't have nearly the influence to turn half the village against their lord.

Once he found Mama, he'd turn to hunting down the source of the unrest. But in the meantime, there had to be another way to appease the people. "I will not paint this killing as anything other than what it is. If anyone asks, this was the work of a wild animal. We'll send out hunting parties. There is no further need to investigate."

Stryjek gave him a polite but facetious smile.

"Right, of course. They'll just forget about it. What do I know?" With a wink, he then folded his hands behind his head and strolled from the room, whistling softly to himself.

When the door closed after him, Kaspian bolted out of Tata's wing-backed chair as if he'd been burned. He turned the key in the lock. Just in case someone did try to come to his office, they'd have to get through a heavy oaken door.

He grasped at his collar and pulled.

Riot. He puffed. It wouldn't come to that. In time, he'd find an explanation, something that would placate the restless people.

For now, he needed a distraction. Hidden behind a stack of books on a nearby shelf were Tata's private stores of gorzałka.

Kaspian pulled out a glass and a bottle, poured a shot, and gulped it down. The pleasant burn ran down into his chest, warming him. He leaned against the shelf, the bottle gripped loosely in his hand.

The villagers wanted answers, but he had none for them. The only thing he knew for certain was Brygida couldn't have done this. That begged the question: what had?

Those footprints in the snow were nothing like he'd seen before. The claw imprints had been the size of his hand, the indentation the size of his forearm. It must have been massive, whatever it was. Brygida would know, but he dared not risk going to her now. The village was watching, and out for blood.

His hands shook, and he balled them into fists.

Stryjek was right, of course. The easiest thing to do would be to deliver the village a scapegoat. He would never turn over Brygida, of course, but even if he did find someone to take the blame, that wouldn't bring Mama back. Wherever she was, whatever had happened to her, that was what he needed to find. Whether person or animal, whatever was responsible for the abduction of the village's beloved Lady Rubin would sate the peasants' lust for vengeance.

If only he could find a clue, something to lead him to her whereabouts.

Feet leaden, he plodded back to the desk and poured another glass, which he drained. The burning had numbed some, and his head was becoming pleasantly light.

Fidgeting with the bottle, Kaspian paced the length of the study, abandoning the glass and taking swigs straight from the bottle. His restless stride brought him to the fireplace, where as he drank, he contemplated the dancing flames.

If he could show them how wonderful Brygida was, share with them all the good the witches did for the village, perhaps they'd learn to love her as much as he did...

A soft knock at the door, and Kaspian groaned.

"I'm not taking any more visitors," he snapped over his shoulder.

The knock persisted. His father was dying, his mother was missing, he was barely holding the bloodthirsty village together without sacrificing the woman he loved, and he couldn't get a moment's peace?

With an angry thump, he set the bottle on the desk and threw open the door.

Stefan and Brygida stood in the hall, and his best friend had the smuggest, most mischievous grin on his face. "Not taking any more visitors, eh?"

"Hello," Brygida whispered, the corners of her lips turning up slightly.

His chest warmed as her violet eyes scanned the room just beyond him. It was always jarring to see her indoors—she belonged in the wild beauty of the forest. The locks, doors, rooms, and other constraints of the village and the indoors were cursed shackles, ones he'd never want to see her in.

These lifeless and orderly shelves were a dull muted gray next to her vibrancy, even just standing still as she was. There was something restless about her, nonetheless, a shifting in her gaze, the way she chewed her lip. Her vibrancy was one of the things he liked best about her; no matter how many times he tried to capture her image in his mind or on canvas, he found something new about her. She was always changing, never the same, and brimming with a life that haloed her beyond the form of her body.

"Are you going to let us in, or are you waiting for the maid to come around and find us?" Stefan asked with a raised eyebrow.

He shook his head to clear it and stepped aside so they could enter.

"You shouldn't be here. It's dangerous," he said to Brygida. Then to Stefan, he said, "Are you insane? Why did you bring her here? Half the village thinks she killed that farmhand, and if they catch her here..."

If the peasants found out, they would form a mob and storm the gates. Just the thought made his blood run cold. Would he have the wherewithal to protect her, or would he crumble as he had that day on the roadside? Although Brygida was powerful, she wasn't infallible. She couldn't use her magic on women; a mob could overwhelm her, pin her down, and hurt her. He'd never forgive himself if she were harmed.

Brygida shook her head, tossing her hair around her face. "It's not Stefan's fault. I came here to ask if I could borrow something of your mother's."

Kaspian's mouth fell open. She wanted to borrow something of Mama's?

"I told you you'd want to talk to her." Stefan grinned.

At least someone found this amusing. At any minute, one of the guards or worse, a peasant might arrive, and it wouldn't be long before the entire village found out she was here. All while they wasted time on jokes.

"This isn't the time for nonsense. I have to get you back home before it's too late." Kaspian headed for the door, to make sure the coast was clear. If they had to, he could sneak her out the window, but it was a long drop from here.

Brygida held up her hand, her fingertips black, even her nails. "I was marked by a demon. I have to find it and kill it before its mark reaches my heart. I believe the same demon has taken your mother, and I need something of hers to help me track them down."

He blinked a few times, trying to clear his vision. But no matter how he tried, the results were the same. Brygida's onyx fingers looked to be carved from stone, and the same creature that had attacked Brygida had attacked his mother? Was she alive, or had she suffered the same sad fate as that peasant?

"Wait." He held up his hands and looked between Brygida and Stefan. "A demon marked you? What does that even mean? And what happens when it reaches your heart?"

"I die," she said matter-of-factly.

Perun's bright lightning, was he cursed? Now Brygida... Was everyone he cared about marked by Weles's dark hand? And how could she be so calm in a situation like this? A chill swept over him. This had to be a nightmare. Surely he'd wake up any moment in his bed. He couldn't lose Brygida, too.

"Does the demon have anything to do with the man who was killed?" Stefan asked.

"I believe so. It never should have gotten here in the first place. The forest should have kept it out." A small frown marred her brow as she rubbed her blackened knuckles. "And I'm sorry, Kaspian, but I do think a bies took your mother."

"Is she...?" His mouth wouldn't form the words.

"Last I saw her, she was alive. If I find your mother, I will bring her back with me, I promise." She grabbed his hand and squeezed it.

He clung to her, reluctant to let her go. Brygida could protect herself. She didn't need him, who'd never used his sword outside of practice with the sword master.

But the idea of letting her walk into danger alone, it made his chest ache. And even worse, knowing that this... bies had taken Mama. What if he let her go alone, and then she and Mama died like Roksana?

He'd done enough running away. Mama wouldn't have been in the forest had they not fought, and it was up to him to bring her back.

"I need something of hers, Kaspian," Brygida said, stroking his knuckles with her thumb.

"You'll have me," he said to her. "I'm coming with you."

Brygida looked him up and down. "You are her blood... You should do."

"Wait a minute." Stefan held up his hands and stepped between them both. "You're joking, right? This bies or whatever it is, it tore that man apart, kidnapped Lady Rubin, and its curse is killing Brygida. And you're just gonna go chasing after it?" His eyebrows shot up to his hairline.

"It's my mother. I can't sit by and just wait." Besides, Brygida was chasing after it. They'd be safer together, wouldn't they?

Stefan shook his head. "Maybe I should expect this sort of thing from you. After all, you did try to give yourself over to that lake skeleton."

"Rusałka," Brygida corrected with a testy smile.

"Yeah, don't want to upset the man-eating fish," Stefan teased.

"Nor Her faithful." Brygida leaned toward Stefan and clicked her teeth pointedly, earning a gape and a quick apology.

Kaspian shuddered. At times he envied Stefan's ability to make light of the situation. But he could remember the cold touch of the rusałki, and the scent of lake water still made him want to retch. How much worse would this bies be?

Perhaps it was better not to think about it, or he'd lose his nerve.

"You don't have to come, I don't expect you to—" Kaspian began to say to Stefan.

Stefan slapped him hard on the back, nearly knocking the wind out of him. "Don't even waste your breath trying to stop me from joining you. Someone has to follow you and make sure you don't get in Brygida's way."

Kaspian forced a smile. Perun's bright lightning, he must be mad to throw himself into danger this way. But whether it was a fool's errand or not, he couldn't stand back anymore while those he cared about were in danger.

He would save Mama, no matter the cost.

CHAPTER 11

Brygida followed Kaspian down the corridor toward the large hall where they'd celebrated Kolęda. He put his hand up, signaling for her to stop.

They were to meet Stefan in the stable, with the supplies from the kitchen. The pack on her shoulders was weighed down with food and water that would last them several days. Mokosza willing, their hunt wouldn't take that long.

The last obstacle was getting past the rest of the household without raising suspicion. The myriad voices of the villagers within the main hall carried beyond its walls.

What would the villagers do if they saw her? She could hold her own against them, but she didn't want to fight them. If they only ever feared her, they would never accept her as part of their community.

A long shadow fell on the wooden floor, drawing closer. Kaspian guarded her with an arm, urging her backward. But as the shadow approached the arched doorway out of the main hall, the paws of a large white dog appeared... The same one that had lain at Lady Rubin's feet during Kolęda?

The dog turned large brown eyes to Brygida and gave a small woof, waving a very furry white tail just slightly.

"Iskra, quiet." Kaspian craned his neck to glance down both directions of the corridor.

Iskra barked again, louder this time, and bounded for the door.

"What's gotten into you?" Kaspian shook his head.

If this was Lady Rubin's dog, perhaps she was worried about her mistress? "I think she wants to come with us."

"We can't bring her. Iskra is an old dog and spends most of the day sleeping." Kaspian's gaze flickered toward the hall. "I don't think she has it in her to take on any adventure bigger than breakfast."

Iskra barked again, more insistently this time, as she paced back and forth in front of the oaken door.

"Seems she disagrees with your assessment," Brygida whispered.

Voices approached from the main hall. It was either bring Iskra or be seen by the villagers.

Brygida opened the door, and Iskra ran out, her white fur nearly indistinguishable from the snow that covered the yard beyond. She buried her black nose in the snow, then popped her head up, sending puffs of white flying.

"I think she's decided for herself," Brygida said with a smile.

With an amused shrug, Kaspian followed her down the stairs, watching Iskra skeptically, as if he doubted his own eyes.

In the barn, they met with Stefan, who had the horses saddled. After they loaded their bags, she climbed into Demon's saddle and they headed toward the snow-laden field where she'd left Halina. Across the snowdrifts and skirting the outbuildings, Iskra followed them.

From a distance, there was no sign of Halina, just a row of dormant trees, their branches dusted with white.

The blackmark itched, and she clenched her jaw. Had Halina abandoned her? Without Halina, she—and now Kaspian and Stefan as well—would have no chance against the bies's mind control.

As she approached, Halina stepped out from behind the trees, her hard expression stony, bow in hand but not drawn. Wind whipped the ever-changing shape of the snow mounds, picking up flakes to rise between them like an ethereal wall. Strands of Halina's auburn hair pulled loose from her braid and fluttered around her face.

Iskra gave Halina a half-hearted bark. Kaspian pulled on the reins of his horse and stayed back, eyeing Halina warily.

Halina sized them up. Her sharp eyes narrowed, and she kept her bow at the ready. She wouldn't use that against them, would she? "I never agreed to let men join us, or a dog..."

Kaspian and Stefan would never hurt either of them, but Halina didn't know that, and hadn't seemed keen on taking her word thus far. She'd have to appeal to Halina's reason.

"They've got horses and supplies that we'll need." She patted Demon's neck. He tossed his head and stamped his hooves. "Besides, they're good with swords and can protect themselves." She'd never seen Stefan use a sword in a fight, or Kaspian for that matter, but they did have them. Kaspian had mentioned he'd been trained by a sword master, so presumably that meant he knew how to use it.

Neither of them spoke. That didn't help.

"You realize the more distractions we bring, the slower we'll move and the faster that"—Halina pointed at Brygida's blackened hand—"progresses to her heart."

There was sense to Halina's words, but it was Kaspian's mother who was missing. How could she tell him no? Besides, she'd gotten something of Lady Rubin's—her son. Tracking the bies would be possible now. This was Weles's test for her, and as she'd done her duty to Mokosza by finding Roksana's murderer, she would find both Lady Rubin and the bies before it was too late.

"I won't get in your way," Kaspian said. "But my mother is in a demon's clutches and Brygida's life is at stake. I won't sit around in my father's study and entertain complaints while they're in danger."

Halina sniffed. His concerns seemed to rank low on her list of priorities. But thanks to him, they'd make much better progress.

Taking hold of Kaspian's hand, Brygida closed her eyes and listened to the flow of his blood, the way it called to his kin—his father and his uncle in the manor house, and the faint whispers leading away, one toward the forest. She pointed a finger in its direction. "I think that's the way leading to Lady Rubin."

"We've wasted enough time," Halina replied. "Let's go." She dug her heels into her mount's side, and they raced forward.

Brygida gave Kaspian an apologetic smile before they took off after her.

Halina set a grueling pace through the deep snow. They stayed off the roads, which meant riding through the woods. Demon at first seemed eager to bolt and resisted her commands, attempting to steer them toward open spaces where he could canter, but Halina and her mare were always right in his way, shepherding him back.

Their winding path brushed her against branches overladen with snow, dumping their contents, soaking her clothes and leaving her shivering.

"Can we stop?" Kaspian called ahead to Halina. "At least for a change of clothes. Brygida is unused to riding, and the snow has—"

"No," Halina called back, without turning around.

Grimacing, Kaspian opened his mouth, but Brygida reached out toward his elbow. As his face turned to hers, his grimace softened a little.

"This is more important," she said, holding up her blackmarked hand. She'd withstood the cold before during winters past on her witchlands, but the blackmark was an unknown. There was no telling how it would affect her as it progressed.

Something stirred in his gaze as he looked her over, something painful, but at last he sighed his agreement and looked away.

As the morning wore on into the afternoon, the others made no mention of discomfort, but her thighs were on fire. Other than the brief trips on Halina's mount or that panicked ride atop Demon's back to save Kaspian, she had spent little time in the saddle.

After riding most of the morning, with the occasional break when Halina stopped to examine a track or a broken branch, it had been hours and her backside now throbbed painfully. To distract herself from the pain, she watched the winter forest transform from the familiarity of her witchlands to something recognizable and yet foreign. The trees here were like any other, but these towering oaks and majestic pines were strangers to her. The same river that ran through her witchlands had frozen over here and sparkled in the noon-day sun, wrong somehow.

The atmosphere here was charged, too. Her eyes darted around, seeking out the source of the feeling of foreboding that had settled in her chest.

Iskra lowered her fluffy white tail and growled, only for a moment, before looking to Kaspian, blinking over shining dark eyes.

Halina fell back to ride beside Brygida. "Do you feel that?"

"I do."

Halina glanced around. "This forest isn't sleeping anymore. We need to be careful."

The trees rustled, despite the absence of wind. And unlike the trees in her witchlands, none of these branches were covered in snow, despite the thick layers covering the ground. She nodded and reached for her scythe. A sleeping forest had apparitions from time to time, dreams, but few demons that would harm humans. However, a waking forest's dreams and nightmares came to life, and their only hope was that this one's sleep hadn't been fitful.

As they made their way through a dense copse of trees, their party was forced apart. Demon took the path around to the left, while Halina, Kaspian, and Stefan took to the right. A cold wind blew, sending a frigid chill through her as it penetrated her damp sleeve. Kaspian reached for his sword, and Stefan scanned their surroundings uneasily.

Light played through the leafless canopy, the barren branches reaching for one another, knotting together like tangled threads and casting long, fractured shadows on the frost. She was nearly around the copse, and only a few feet separated her from the others.

Stefan raised his head, a faint smile on his lips. "At least it's sunny for once."

She began to smile, too, but... the direction of the shadows wasn't right. She glanced overhead.

This light was from another source.

She whipped her head around—

Kaspian's gaze fixated on the sparkling ice, their blue slowly fading to dullness.

This was the light of a *błędnica*. A demon. They appeared as orbs of light, will-o-wisps, false forms that led travelers down false trails, right into freezing deaths or the maws of waiting predators.

There was no way to fight them, not even with magic.

"Halina!" Brygida attuned to the scythe's whispering, weaving into the same intention, raising the snow from the ground in a wall that towered high before them, and arced overhead, blotting out the light. "Lead them away!"

"Brygida!" Kaspian protested, but Stefan grabbed his horse's reins, leading them both behind Halina.

Iskra shot ahead of them all, a blurry ball of fur, guiding their escape.

A błędnica could be bribed with gifts, especially gifts of rich food and drink... but, at least as far as Mama had told her, no one who'd ever seen one directly in her true form had ever lived to tell the tale...

CHAPTER 12

The wall of ice broke the błędnica's mesmerizing for the moment. Quickly, Brygida dismounted and pulled out a wrapped bundle of smoked venison Mamusia had packed for her. Demon screamed, but she held a finger to her lips, uttering a soothing sound.

He clopped his hooves in the snow but quieted.

Approaching the wall of ice, she came face to face with frost-white eyes and matching hair in enormous cascades. Pale bare skin shimmered on a perfect feminine body. Feet capped in crystalline nails slowly neared the translucent barrier.

Lowering her gaze, Brygida let a doorway dissolve in the ice, and the spicy scent of cloves tickled her nostrils. Keeping her eyes from the błędnica's face, she bowed. "Forest spirit, woodland wanderer, lady of the trees, we humbly make you an offering of nourishment and ask for safe passage through your realm."

She knelt in the snow and reverently placed the wrapped bundle, bowing low, touching her forehead to the cold ground, shivering in the silence.

Whether a bundle of smoked venison would be rich enough to spare their group, she didn't know. But it was their only hope.

Her heart rose into her throat, beating wildly in the quiet, until soft footsteps crunched in the snow.

A shadow darkened over her.

She trembled uncontrollably, the tiny hairs on the back of her neck standing on end.

The shadow grew... and then it was gone.

She dared not rise, not yet, but the shadows on the ground were once more short noon-day shadows. The unnatural light had disappeared.

Maybe a little lift. She raised her chin, just enough.

The wrapped bundle was gone, and only slender footprints remained.

The błędnica had accepted their offering.

A relieved sigh rippled from her lips, and she looked over her shoulder at Demon. He tossed his head and shifted his dark forelock out of his eye.

She stood on trembling legs. As she retreated back to him, she grasped onto his neck to hold her up, leaning her face into his mane. She'd dealt with demons before, but she didn't have Mama's or Halina's immunity to them, and outside her witchlands, in a waking forest, she was out of her depth. She had to count on the knowledge her mothers had handed down to her, and on Halina's guidance, to get through this.

Thank you, Mama and Mamusia. You've saved me yet again.

A bark echoed from behind a cluster of pines. She had to find the others.

She tried to climb into Demon's saddle, but her blackmarked arm went limp and she slid back to the ground. She stared at her trembling limb. Was this the effect of the blackmark or her rattled nerves?

Demon lowered for her, bowed and waiting. With a whisper of gratitude, she mounted up, then followed the trails of hoofprints the others had left.

Ahead, Kaspian paced a furrow in the snow, raking a gloved hand through his hair. Against the black sable fur of his cloak, his blond was a light amber, a dreamy summer wheat field. His hand took turns hovering over the hilt of his sword and clenching into a fist. No matter that he was trained in combat, a heart like his should manifest in strokes of the brush and emotion captured in paint, not bloody slashes of a blade.

"I'm going to look for her," Kaspian bit out to Halina.

"You'd be useless against the błędnica. She's Ewa's daughter. She can take care of herself." Bow clutched in hand, Halina stared him down.

"But it's not only that. What about the—"

"*Mamon,*" Halina provided with a yawn.

"Look." Stefan waved toward her. Next to him, Iskra lay in the snow, practically indistinguishable from its immaculate white but for her dark nose and eyes.

Kaspian paused in his constant pacing, lowered his hands, and took a few steps toward her. "You're safe," he breathed, and trudged to her through the snow to grip Demon's bridle. "Are you all right?"

Halina rolled her eyes. "I told him you knew what to do, but it did not stop this one from slowly tunneling into the earth with his maddening restlessness."

Kaspian returned the look and shook his head. "We ran into this part-bull, part-dog beast that thought we wanted to steal its hoard of coins?" He frowned, as if trying to make sense of it. "But Halina just allowed the will-o-wisps to lead us away, at least far enough to placate the beast. I wanted to make sure you didn't wander into the... mamon's territory unbeknown."

That had been considerate of him. She grasped his hand and gave it a squeeze.

But Halina had done well. It was far simpler to recede from a mamon's territory and leave it be than to remain, or worse approach and risk its ire, along with a fierce defense of its hoard. If Halina hadn't been with them, Kaspian and Stefan could have been in danger as she'd dealt with the błędnica. They'd barely entered these woods and had already encountered multiple demons and spirits.

Halina shrugged a shoulder and raised an eyebrow at her.

Stefan cleared his throat. "Perhaps we should seek shelter? I, for one, do not want to have another run-in with a demon. Halina mentioned something about a witch living here?"

"Yes. Her name is Anita," Halina replied, "and her cottage is nearby. If anyone has answers about what's going on here, it's her." Despite that good news, Halina's low voice and drooped gaze said otherwise.

Mamusia had taught her that as long as a witch was on her witchlands, the forest should remain slumbering. And yet this one was waking. The creeping dread when they'd first entered these woods now wrapped her tight.

Before she could voice her concerns, Halina clucked to her horse and turned around, leading the way past frost-coated shrubs and boulders deeper into the forest. Kaspian exchanged a questioning look with her before giving Demon a final pat and returning to his own mount.

She joined him and Stefan, and the three of them followed Halina, scanning their wooded surroundings. No one said a word to interrupt the soft clop of hooves or the rare hiss of wind through leafless tree limbs. Only the quiet crunch of Iskra's slow steps in the snow and the tumble of accumulation from branches to the forest floor dared sound.

Holding the Scythe of the Mother close, she remained attuned to its innumerable voices, listening for warnings, for advice, for any wisdom the old blood of Mrok witches could offer. But the voices had hushed to sparse whispers, lilting, uncertain, as if they awaited some wisdom from her.

Her hand ached, as if bitten by cold, or burning as it did after chopping wood for hours or grinding herbs. Had her predecessors been tested by Weles in this way as well?

Or was she the first Mrok witch to take the Scythe of the Mother outside of their witchlands? Had anyone ever taken it outside of that wood and Czarnobrzeg, by every other name it had ever borne?

And her witchlands, they... they had no name. No Mrok witch had ever been so arrogant as to name the forest, to overbear as if to own, for although the witchlands were hers, they were hers as a mother was hers. Hers to belong to.

Would the witch this forest claimed be like her, like her mothers? Apart from them and the occasional huntress like Halina, she'd never met another witch. And the excitement she would have felt was tempered by her uneasiness.

But if the forest had awoken, something terrible must have happened, and the mere thought of her mothers potentially facing that catastrophe too made her shudder. She was here to heal the mark of the bies and to find Lady Rubin, but as was her duty to Mokosza, she would do all she could to help this forest and its witch.

At the front, Halina held up a hand, and they all stopped. She clenched Demon's reins tighter. What was wrong?

Ahead was a cottage, not unlike the one she and her mothers inhabited. A thatch roof and a single dark window faced them, a bit smaller than theirs; the garden was larger, surrounded by stacked stone walls and a barren fruit tree that she imagined shaded and cooled the cottage in the summer. But the animal pen was open and empty, and no smoke emanated from the chimney. In this weather, the inside had to be frigid.

As Halina dismounted, she cleared the view of the cottage's doorway. Its open doorway. Snow piled up and over the threshold.

Something twisted in her chest, and her heartbeat throbbed too close to the skin, pebbling her flesh. The trees were too close here, their roots reaching for the house as if to reclaim it, the sense of eyes on her in the woods too keen. What had happened to wake this forest?

Halina ran toward the door.

Brygida swung out of the saddle too and moved to follow Halina, but Kaspian put his hand on her arm.

"Don't," he whispered, his mouth downturned. Somber.

Then he believed he knew what was in that cottage. The very thing she didn't want to believe.

"I'm going in there. There's a chance I can help." She hefted her scythe.

He shook his head sadly, but his hand slipped down her arm. "What awaits in there, only Weles can help."

The eerie whispers rose in the Scythe of the Mother, competing for air. *Don't go... Go... She's not there. The forest, it's awake... The awakening... She's not there. You can't help. Go. Go...*

She frowned. Before, when she'd acted as Mokosza's Reaper of Death, the scythe had spoken in unison to her, a chorus of voices guiding her path, but now... They were torn.

But she would go inside. She had to.

The open doorway called to her, black as night against a field of winter. Squinting to see inside, she moved toward it and stepped in, where the voices of her scythe hushed to a chilling quiet.

CHAPTER 13

The snow caked on Brygida's boots slid off in sheaves of white onto the black.

Within, everything was black. The black hearth held no fire. The black table had been overturned. Black dishes and black jars lay in pieces upon the black floor.

It was wrong. Everything was wrong.

Halina stood in the center of it all, her hands on her head. She stumbled back, revealing Mokosza's altar burned to ash. And on the floor, discarded like playthings, the yarns on a Belt of the Golden Spider were scorched, a Scythe of the Mother broken in half. Her heart caught in her throat.

This place—it was just like the cottage she shared with her mothers.

In the blizzard, it had been cloaked in white, its charred remnants hidden, but inside...

"Did a demon do this?" Kaspian asked from behind her, standing outside the doorway. He hadn't entered, and somehow it felt just like him to abstain out of respect.

"No. This was villagers." Halina picked up the soot-stained Mokosza's Spider from the belt, her fingers caressing it lovingly. "I shouldn't have left her alone," Halina said, covering her mouth.

Villagers had done this?

She was far from home, but it was easy to imagine the village near here wasn't much different than Czarnobrzeg. People just like them lived right outside her witchlands.

How could they?

She didn't want to believe it, but after the Rubin guards had drawn swords on her, she hadn't the heart to object. There were some in Czarnobrzeg too, like Dariusz, who would doubtless rejoice at any harm befalling her.

But where was Anita? Although the cottage was in ruins, there was no sign of her, dead or alive. What if she had fled, and they had only burned her cottage?

But given Halina's reaction, perhaps there was a piece she was missing...

"Did you know her well?" Brygida asked softly.

For a long while, Halina remained silent, only

stroking Mokosza's Spider, but then very slowly, she nodded her head.

"We'd met a few times over the years. She was an older witch, with no daughter to follow in her footsteps. Last time I saw her, she mentioned that the villagers nearby had been acting strange. I offered to help, to give her protection, but she assured me she could take care of it herself. She trusted them, and I trusted her. But their kind are never to be trusted—I should have known better."

Kaspian shifted uncomfortably behind her.

Still, if Halina believed the villagers had killed Anita —how? What could they have possibly done to defeat a witch on her witchlands? "How could villagers do that? What about the wrath of the blood?"

Halina puffed bitterly. "You underestimate what their kind are capable of, maleńka. We are powerful, but we are still human, and we still bleed."

Her fingertips tingled, and she looked down at her blackmarked hand. Finding this burnt cottage, it couldn't be a coincidence. The gods sent messages in many ways. Was this a warning? She pulled her scythe closer.

"I would never harm Brygida," Kaspian said.

"And what of your neighbors, your family, your friends?" Halina looked at Stefan, who straightened, a sober expression on his face, but neither of them could face her.

"That's what I thought. One wolf that doesn't kill you says nothing of the rest."

It wasn't like that, she wanted to say. But Mama's grip on her arm still smarted, as did her many warnings over the years. Mamusia had kept her confined to their witchlands for nearly her entire life, too.

They all had Mokosza's divine power, but it was a gift and not a right. They were forbidden from harming spiders, ravens, sheep, and women, all of which were under Her protection. Had a mob of women and men come for Anita, and had she hesitated, preferring to honor Mokosza's orders over her own life?

But why would the villagers turn on her?

As a Reaper of Death, she'd commanded the village's respect, but could that respect be twisted into fear? A fear great enough to kill Mokosza's Hand?

She had Mama and Mamusia to guide her and keep her safe, but this solitary witch, Anita, what had her life been like? Had she suffered the uneasiness, the fear, alone? Had she pretended it didn't exist? Had she truly trusted the villagers the way Mama had always warned not to?

A lump formed in her throat as she clutched her vial of lake water. A part of her had always seen herself as untouchable, blessed by the power given to her by Mokosza. But what if this witch had thought the same and died for it?

Halina knelt before the altar, head bowed in prayer.

Brygida too approached the burnt altar, brushed off the debris, and then rested the remaining charred threads of the belt along with the broken scythe upon it.

The voices in her Scythe of the Mother had been many, countless, offering their wisdom and their questions, their power and their fear, all of which had helped her when she'd been in need. And this witch's scythe had meant no less. To leave it lying on the floor, broken, brought it none of the respect and kindness it deserved.

She rested a hand on it. *Scythe of the Mother, thank you for your guidance over countless lifetimes. May the witches you've guided and the lives you've saved find you in the world beyond.*

A soft, pained harmony of moans answered.

"Brygida—" Halina began, her voice softer than before.

If there is anything I can do to help—

An aura of soft white light glowed around the pieces of the broken scythe.

She gasped, scrambling to her feet as ghostly, ethereal faces emerged from its light, flowing toward one another. Dozens fled the broken pieces, a cloud of phantoms bursting forth, surging between them.

Agog, all she could do was watch until the last spirit absorbed into the unity, and the light faded from the broken pieces. They released what sounded like a breath, and then the space between them became water. It filled in every break, every crack, shone a blinding white.

And then the Scythe of the Mother was whole.

The remaining water formed a puddle on the altar, sparkling in the sparse remaining light, and overflowed down the sides, leaving streaks of clean ash wood.

No one said a word, standing in silent awe.

Mokosza had just repaired Anita's scythe, clear as day. And what voices and power it had contained had spoken.

Brygida stared at the second Scythe of the Mother, unblinking.

Halina gasped. "I've never seen..." Her words drifted off.

She wasn't sure what to call it either. Did Mamusia's grimoire contain any wisdom on this? As she took a step back, the floorboard creaked beneath her foot, sending up a puff of ash at the edges.

His eyebrows knitted together, Kaspian slowly approached it and descended to a knee, pulling a hunting knife from his belt. He wedged it into the edge and pried the floorboard off.

Beneath lay a shrunken, curled leather sack. Wordlessly, she reached for it.

Inside was Anita's grimoire.

The feeling of unease continued to crawl over Brygida's skin. Inside the grimoire could be the answer to what had happened to Anita.

But it was intimate, more so than a journal, yet it would be cold somehow to leave it beneath the cottage, where looters or others untrained in the path could find it. Anita had no successor, but her Scythe of the Mother had spoken as clear an answer as they'd ever get.

It also didn't feel right to open Anita's grimoire here in front of all the others. Something horrible had happened here, and staying wasn't an option. They'd have to find other shelter, and that meant taking the grimoire with her.

"I'm assuming we won't be staying here," Stefan said, somber eyes scanning over the charred remains of Anita's home.

Iskra whined, as if to add her vote to his.

"We need to talk," Halina said. "Alone." She gave a pointed look to Kaspian and Stefan, who lingered just outside the threshold.

Kaspian made a show of looking around the area. "We'll give you some privacy."

With a nod from Brygida, the two men rode out with Iskra, and aside from their receding steps, stillness and quiet reclaimed the wood. It felt wrong to send them away in these restless woods, even if they remained in view just at the edge of the clearing.

Before she left the burnt cottage, she reverently placed Anita's Scythe of the Mother in the hiding place beneath the floorboards. If another witch ever did protect these witchlands, she would need it.

Finished, Brygida headed outside. The weight of innumerable eyes were upon her, the restlessness crawling under her skin, and she wouldn't feel safe again until they were out of these tainted witchlands. Or until she found out what had really happened to Anita.

CHAPTER 14

Brygida rubbed her arms and eyed Halina. "What did you want to talk to me about?"

Halina's gaze trailed after Kaspian and Stefan, and she didn't look away. "Ewa told me about your relationship with the villager. I understand, believe me," she said, lowering her chin with a fleeting wistful smile. "The men from the village are fun for a while, but... their use is limited."

Brygida blushed. "I don't know what you're implying."

"That man over there—" Halina blew out a breath. "He'll be sweet to you... until he gets what he wants. But after that, you'll be nothing to him."

"Kaspian's not like that." Brygida shook her head. Mama had said the same, but Kaspian hadn't pushed for anything more than enjoying one another's company. She'd never even known a man before him, and he understood that. If he'd pursued her because he was in a hurry and wanted... more, well, there were plenty of agreeable women in the village he would've pursued instead.

Someday she'd be ready. Someday she'd have to be —Mama and Mamusia had only her to carry on the Mrok line. But that day was far from now, and Kaspian respected that.

"They're all the same," Halina replied with a dismissive wave, her eagle-sharp eyes narrowed. "There's a certain allure to us because we're different, but in the dark, once they get their hands on us, they realize it's all the same. And when we become inconvenient, this is what happens." She gestured in the direction of the destroyed cottage.

That would never happen. Kaspian had always defended her and her mothers, had kept the villagers from trying to do them harm. He'd never neglect that duty, let alone allow something like this to happen to them. "You don't know him like I do."

"That mark isn't going to slow down." Halina gestured to it. "It's already up past your wrist."

It had indeed spread farther. And its tingling only got worse the longer she stood here, radiating through her fingers, hand, and wrist like thunderbolts. She hid her hand in her cloak.

"Hide it all you want, but you know your days are

numbered. And as for Anita, I've seen things like this before. It spreads like a disease. Your man and his comrade aren't special. They'll hear something from the wrong lips, and they'll turn on us both. Witches will scream their last all across the region, if not all of Nizina. If you want to live, then you need to come with me. Alone."

Alone? "Without Kaspian, we have no way of tracking Lady Rubin, or the bies. I'm as good as dead without him," she said. "And besides, they're my friends. They wouldn't hurt me, or you."

"We could take the dog. It belonged to the village woman, didn't it?" Halina whipped her auburn braid over her shoulder. "And your 'friends' are going to get you killed. I promised Ewa I would help you remove the blackmark, but I won't stick around to get shackled in my sleep and burned at the stake because some malaise spread through the sheep herds, or someone's fruit preserves spoiled in the cellar." Halina gave a half-hearted shrug, then looked back the way they'd come. "If you give your trust so easily, sister, at least be sure to watch your back."

Halina was leaving? Just like that? After seeing what had been done to Anita, her confidence had broken.

But without Halina, could she protect herself, or Kaspian and Stefan for that matter? Her heart caught in her throat. "How will I fight the bies without you?"

"You don't have to. Come with me if you don't want to figure it out on your own. "

Kaspian and Stefan lingered at the edge of the wood, glancing back in her direction. Kaspian, who was counting on her to find his mother. Without Halina, they'd be less familiar with the land, less equipped to handle any demons, at a disadvantage both in knowledge and ability.

But it was Kaspian's blood that sang to that of Lady Rubin the strongest, and her surest way of finding the bies. She grasped her vial of lake water with her black-marked hand. The tingling faded.

She was a Mrok witch, and she'd found Julian against all odds.

She was a skilled tracker—Mama had taught her well.

And she'd have to kill the bies herself to heal the mark.

She didn't know Halina very well, but when Lady Rubin was in danger, Halina had left her for dead. And she claimed to have offered Anita protection, but what if she had seen her as a lost cause and had abandoned her to her fate as well?

For Halina, when it came down to her life or another, there was little doubt which Halina would choose. Kaspian, however, had been willing to give himself over to the rusałki to save her and the village. Stefan had valiantly tried to defend him at the crossroads from the mob. They were brave, devoted, and true friends.

If she had to choose between going with Halina or staying with her friends, the choice was clear. "Thank you for all your help thus far. I'm going to stay here with my friends."

With an exasperated sigh, Halina shook her head. "Suit yourself. By Her thread, Brygida."

"By Her thread." She lowered her chin in parting as Halina turned her horse around and rode away. She disappeared into snow-covered pines without a sound.

Crestfallen, she led Demon toward Kaspian and Stefan. "We should leave this place."

"What about Halina?" A line etched between Kaspian's pale eyebrows.

"We've... decided to part ways." She wasn't about to mention that Halina suspected they'd murder her in her sleep.

"Shame. Her constant frown was so pleasant." Stefan smiled sardonically.

His joke was well founded, but she couldn't return the smile. Doing so in this place felt wholly wrong.

Her hand tightened around the grimoire once more. Losing Halina was unexpected, but hopefully Anita's grimoire held answers.

Stefan looked away, his mouth downturned.

"Shall we?" Kaspian prompted.

"Yes." She wanted to get out of this waking forest as soon as possible.

They got back onto their horses and rode on, following the hum of Kaspian's blood tie. Her gaze was continually drawn back to the burnt cottage until it shrank from view, swallowed up by trees and snow.

Through the twisting pathways, she did her best to lead them down the meandering trails out of the forest by using animal tracks as their guide. But the light of day was dying, and they were in desperate need of shelter.

"Oh, gods. Does this forest ever end?" Stefan mumbled, slumping in the saddle.

Her sore backside couldn't agree more. But she wouldn't stop until they were out of the waking wood.

"Are you regretting joining me?" Kaspian teased him.

"Just that?" Stefan shook his head. "I'm a fool for ever befriending you, lordling."

A grin lit Kaspian's face, and despite the horrors of today, her own face brightened.

A scream rent the air.

By the Mother—

The bies? It had to be.

But a woman's voice—

Kaspian took off in its direction immediately. She dug her heels into Demon's sides and shot forward too, following the sound of a woman's screams.

CHAPTER 15

Kaspian's racing heart thundered in his ears. Mama was in danger. She could be dying. And he wouldn't slow down until he got to her.

A thick trail of blood swathed the snow, in places smeared by massive paw prints. He slowed, following the trail with a twisting pain in his chest.

The farther he went, the more the crimson mixed with burgundy, older darker blood. This was a place of death, and had been for a long time.

Was Mama's blood staining this snow? Could the scream they'd heard have been hers? Or was this the lifeblood of some other unfortunate soul?

The gruesome tracks stopped at the gaping mouth of a cave atop a small hill. Gray icicles lined the roof, like the fangs of a beast, and below, muddled bloody footprints.

The hairs on the back of his neck stood on end. The air here was charged, dangerous and foreboding. This was the den of a predator.

Or a bies.

Hands slick with sweat, he grasped the hilt of his sword and drew it. He'd never killed with it before, but Perun's bright lightning, if a bies had his mother, tonight his blade would taste blood.

A guttural scream ripped through the air, followed by the low mournful howl of the bies.

Perun, give me strength.

"Kaspian!" Brygida's voice.

He looked over his shoulder at her, at the determined set of her brow. Power rippled from her in waves, her eyes brighter, burning and fierce, and the vial around her neck sparkled like starlight. Iskra was at her side, tail low, growling.

He wasn't alone. Together with Brygida and Stefan, they could face this bies and save Mama.

"You two just keep it distracted long enough for me to kill it," Brygida said, with all the authority of a guard captain. "If you look in its eyes, it may try to control you, so be careful."

Kaspian nodded, his throat too tight to form any words. This was it. Into the bies's den. Brygida and

Stefan hid behind a fallen tree, and with a loaded glance from Brygida, so did Iskra.

Crouching low to the ground, Kaspian moved behind a ragged bosk. It didn't conceal much, but then, his job was to be seen. One hand grasping the hilt of his sword, he snapped a branch off a bush and tossed it toward the mouth of the cave.

It struck an icicle with a soft clink.

The sharp spike fell to the ground, shattering to pieces, the sound echoing back at him, amplified by the cave.

Inside the depths of the shadows, a lumbering figure stirred.

Across the way, Stefan crept around the other side of the cave, and with a large fallen branch, he rapped hard against the ground.

A thump, and the pat of claws on stone drew closer.

Kaspian broke a few twigs, giving his position away. *Come out here, monster.* He kept making noise while Stefan moved into position.

Stefan scrambled up the side of the hill and over the mouth of the cave, then at its peak, he squatted and unsheathed his sword.

From the darkness beneath, a wolf-life muzzle covered in thick, wiry black hair emerged, its black-gray lip curled back to reveal pointed teeth as long as fingers.

Stefan met his gaze, a question in his eyes.

With a flicker of a look toward Brygida, who nodded

to him at the base of the hill, Kaspian bobbed his head to Stefan.

Stefan leaped down from above, burying his blade in the demon's back.

It reared, swiping at Stefan with yellowed claws, but Stefan rolled away.

The demon's back to him, Kaspian charged forward and plunged his blade into the demon's side, rending it free to leap away.

He came face to face with a set of sharp white teeth. A second demon had emerged from the cave.

Identical in appearance, it growled and lunged for him.

At the last second, he rolled to the side and scrambled to try to get to his feet, but the snow gave him no purchase. He buried his fingers deep, his nails crushing against hard, cold earth.

Right before his face, water burst up from the ground, knocking the demon aside. All around it, icicles sprang forth like spears, piercing its body, spraying blood against the stark snow.

Kaspian swiveled his head toward Brygida. Water gathered around her like a living cloak. Her scythe in hand, she climbed to the mouth of the cave with eerie serenity, Iskra whining behind her.

"I thought it was just the one demon?" Stefan ran toward him and yanked him to his feet.

Brygida approached the first demon, who raised its

wolfish head from its pool of thick reddish-black blood staining the snow. She glanced at her scythe, and its blade lengthened with sharp, crystalline ice.

With an impossibly adept swing, crimson spattered her face as the demon's head hit the ground.

"*Wilkołak,*" she said icily, peering into the cave. "A man who has become a wolf demon. This isn't the bies that marked me. But their bite can be contagious. Be on your guard."

There was something otherworldly about her when she summoned her magic, but it felt... right, as if it were her truth, the way the gods had intended her.

A howl echoed through the pine trees, joined by another and another and another. More of them?

From out of the winter woods, several *wilkołaki* emerged, moving like black shadows, eyes flashing crimson.

Closing ranks, he and Stefan put their backs to one another, swords out. Brygida surrounded them with a wall of icy water.

There were at least six of them. Could they survive? Would Brygida's power even be enough?

"Well, there's only one way out of this," Stefan murmured.

Brygida nodded.

There was no turning back. The sword in his hand was all he had, and he wouldn't allow another person he loved to be taken away. Wiping his sweaty palms on the front of his coat, he readjusted his grip and planted his feet. It was fight or die, and he wasn't ready to die today.

A wilkołak broke from the pack and circled them on its wolfish paws, coming in close.

With a sweep of Brygida's arm, a bulwark of ice jutted out of the snow. She sent the wilkołak flying over the heads of its packmates. An arc of water droplets sparkled as they froze and fell to the ground.

A second and a third wilkołak attacked simultaneously, flanking them on either side. They were being boxed in.

Kaspian thrust out his sword, but the wilkołak twisted mid-air and he missed it by a hair.

The wilkołaki howled, their voices carrying up to the sky and rattling around in his skull, splitting his mind like a bolt of lightning.

"Get behind me!" Brygida beckoned with her blackmarked hand, the black reaching up to her elbow now.

She grasped for the vial around her neck, her lips moving wordlessly as the wilkołaki closed in around them.

Another one broke from the pack, rushing toward her. Placing himself between her and the wilkołak, he lunged upward as it leaped into the air.

Hot blood sprayed him. His blade embedded deep into the wilkołak's furred chest. It contorted, nearly wrenching his arm. It fell to the ground, bringing him crashing down with it, pinned beneath its weight.

A whooshing sound filled his ears.

Water rushed over him and crashed down before the wilkołaki, knocking them back, sweeping them away like a river overflowing its banks.

The wilkołak atop him attempted to hold on to his arm, but Kaspian angled the point of his blade right for the heart.

The wilkołak cried out, a tormented sound, but its grip didn't relent, even as the wave pulled. This creature wanted to live. This creature had once been a man.

"Kaspian," Brygida warned. "You have to—"

"I know!" He drew his hunting knife and cut at the claws clutching his sleeve before it could bite him and turn him into one of them.

CHAPTER 16

The claws released from Kaspian's sleeve, blood staining his coat as the wilkołak's flagging heartbeat pumped out its life force. Its crimson eyes met his, dimming while the wave bore it away. *May the ravens of Mokosza bear you to your rest...*

Stefan yanked him back, away from the flood wave, and Kaspian watched the water freeze over lifeless bodies on the ground in an instant.

Everything stilled, and as Brygida set foot on the ice, snow spread beneath her steps. With a look at her scythe, its blade lengthened with that same crystalline edge. She approached what bodies remained, swept that massive blade, and severed heads from shoulders.

His bloody hands trembled.

He tried to wipe them clean in the snow, but it had already stained the beds of his fingernails.

Lying on the ground, beheaded, the wilkołaki looked so small and helpless. Stefan removed his blade from a corpse with a wet pop and wiped it off on the snow before sheathing it. Brygida gave a sharp whistle, and Iskra emerged from the bushes and meandered to Stefan. A wound on his leg bled freely.

"Were you bit?" Brygida asked them, so calmly as the bloodied ice blade faded from her scythe.

Stefan tore a strip off his shirt with his teeth and set about tending his wound. "No, cut myself on a dang rock. Nothing I can't manage. You two?"

"I'm all right," she replied, then her gaze wandered from Stefan to him. For a moment, it seemed darker somehow, but then it cleared. "Kaspian? Are you injured?"

She took his hand in hers.

Her blackened hand cupped his bloody one. What a pair they made. He couldn't meet Brygida's eyes, didn't want her to see just how shaken he was. It shouldn't bother him that he'd killed the wilkołak. After all, if he hadn't, it would have killed him. And yet seeing it die, he was cut to the bone. If it had been a person once, had it become a wilkołak willingly? Or had its fate been forced, and now, its death...?

And Brygida? She'd killed as if it were second nature. As if she were slaughtering a chicken for dinner. And she'd done so with a finesse befitting the wild's most skilled predators.

There were peasants who whispered about attacking the witches, but they could only be the fools who hadn't seen her power. Because they didn't realize they were flies—mere flies buzzing about flying directly into the spider's web. She'd dispatched demons with ease. What threat were peasants?

Whatever had claimed Anita's life—despite Halina's suspicions—couldn't have been so simple as a mob of peasants. Brygida was a young witch, and if the older, more experienced Anita had matched even her caliber, that mob would've been no more than prey.

"Kaspian?" Brygida asked softly, blinking over inquisitive eyes.

"I'm fine." He pulled away from her, his gaze following the blood trail in the snow once more. This wasn't the demon that had attacked Brygida and Mama, but he had heard a woman's scream. "We should search the cave for survivors."

He rose on his own power, gathered his composure as best he could, and strode toward the cave. The sickly sweet odor of decaying flesh stopped him short.

"Oh, that's awful," Stefan said.

One hand covering his mouth and nose, Kaspian led the way inside. *Please, Almighty Perun, let Mama be here and alive.*

Something crunched under his feet.

Bones littered the ground, some with strips of rotting flesh clinging to them, others picked clean...

animals, he hoped. His boot collided with a half-consumed human hand.

"Perun's bright lightning, is that—?" His eyes searched for the rest as his mind struggled to comprehend.

"Just keep going." Brygida took the lead, her chin held high and the color bleached from her face. This couldn't be pleasant for her, but she wasn't shrieking at the horror and fleeing either.

He swallowed hard, his stomach in knots as he followed her. Deep in the heart of the cave, the darkness blanketed his head, and he couldn't see a thing.

A soft whimper came from a lump on the ground.

Kaspian fell to his knees beside it, grasping a delicate hand. "Mama?"

It was difficult to discern features in the dark.

"Let's get her out of here," Brygida said.

As he grasped the woman's waist, a wet warmth coated his arm. His heart stuttered in his chest, and the fragile body in his arms trembled. *Please, let it not be too late.*

Rushing into the gray light of day, he couldn't look at the face of the woman in his arms. Her breathing slowed, faded, and then was gone. He clamped his eyes shut.

No. Please.

"Kaspian..." Brygida said gently.

He opened his eyes.

A young woman with golden-blond hair, blue eyes staring up at the sky, unblinking. A bloody gash over her heart. Roksana. He jerked his head back. His breath caught.

No.

A stranger.

Not Mama. But a person, a life.

He let out the breath he'd been holding and lowered the young woman's limp body onto the snow. She'd been too young to die. Just like Roksana.

He looked away. But even averting his gaze couldn't prevent the specter of Roksana's body lying on that table in the forest cottage, her golden hair tangled up in weeds. A warm, wet tongue licked at his cheek, and he let himself lean against Iskra's hulking, furry weight.

"We were too late," Brygida whispered, her voice quivering.

It was the first time he'd heard her that way... and it made his chest ache and his shoulders slump forward.

With her blackened hand, she brushed the golden hair away from the young woman's face. As deadly as she'd been only minutes earlier, she was loving now, caring, mournful.

Somewhere between mankind's primal ancestors to now, the cold pragmatism of nature had died in men, but in Brygida, in her family, it still lived. It thrived.

When it was kill or be killed, she did not waver. And when it came to protecting those her goddess bid her to, she did so with all her heart.

Weles have mercy on the peasants foolish enough to test a witch, for in a clash of their hatred and the witches' power, the victor would be clear and ruthless in battle.

But as powerful as she was, the blackmark was consuming her hand, consuming her. It was eating her alive, and she had only him, Stefan, and herself to find and defeat the bies who'd marked her. And the black-mark was already halfway to her heart.

Time was running out. For Mama and for Brygida both.

AFTER THEY'D BURNED THE WOMAN'S BODY, KASPIAN'S clothes stank like smoke, gore, and Perun only knew what else. Almost a full day had passed and they were no closer to finding answers or finding Mama. The only bright spot was finally escaping the woods, searching out a nearby village to alert about the young woman's death.

In the distance, he spotted a farmhouse, but no smoke rose from the chimney. Perhaps someone lived here that they could give the tragic news to, but night was also closing in; they'd need to find shelter and soon. He would prefer if it was within four walls.

Brygida and Stefan gave him nods, and he urged his horse to canter closer. As he approached, he spotted the open barn doors. Iskra accompanied him, gazing out at the open land, with not even a whisper of a bark.

The snow here was untouched, piled high against a farmhouse. No one had lived here for a while. There were rumors of famine, a crop blight that had left many people struggling to feed themselves in Granat. And because Lord Granat taxed them so heavily, they hadn't even had enough to feed themselves. Where had these people gone? Had they moved on, or had they perished like that witch from the cottage?

Kaspian dismounted and dug out the door with his boot, before pulling it open enough to peer inside. An oaken table at the center, a bed to one side, and a cold hearth and ashes scattered around it. A layer of dust clung to every surface. Iskra slipped inside, trotting around and sniffing. Whoever had lived here was long gone.

He waved Brygida and Stefan closer, and their weary horses trudged through the snow banks to reach him. "No sign of anyone to talk to, but it seems we can stay here for tonight."

There were dark circles beneath Brygida's eyes, and her skin had lost some of its color. It had been a long day for all of them.

Stefan swung down from the saddle, and when he landed on the ground, he winced.

"Are you all right?" Brygida tilted her head to peer at his leg. The wound had soaked through his makeshift bandage and spread to his breeches.

"It's nothing serious, just a deeper gash than I thought." Stefan smiled, but it was strained. The lines around his face were too tight.

"Go inside and tend to your wound. I'll see to the horses." Kaspian nodded toward the cottage.

"Are you sure you can handle it? Demon's a biter, and—"

Kaspian huffed. "I think I can handle some horses. I'm not about to let you bleed out removing tack and pouring feed."

"Best of luck, then." With another pained grimace, Stefan handed the reins to him before taking the shoulder Brygida offered. He limped into the cottage with her, while Kaspian led the horses into the barn.

Inside smelled of damp and rotting hay, and ice coated the ground. Stepping around it carefully, he led the horses into stalls before working his way through unsaddling, feeding, and blanketing the horses as best he could.

He burned the clothes that were the most stained by demonic ichor and washed, if it could be called such, given the limited time and resources. But the stench remained, and it made the horses skittish.

By the time he got to Demon's stall, his back ached. How did Stefan do this all day at the manor?

Demon stamped his hooves and flared his nostrils in displeasure as he danced back and forth in his borrowed stall. He was a temperamental horse on a good day. And whether today was good remained to be seen.

Demon reared, and Kaspian stumbled backward to avoid being knocked by his hooves. "Fine. You want to be that way, then starve."

He slid out of the stable, bucket of oats in hand. He'd hoped it would be enough to pacify Demon into compliance as it had the other two horses, but he'd been wrong. Soothing Demon was Stefan's preserve.

Mama and Tata had always forbidden him from working in the stables, but he'd always stolen away to do it whenever the chance had arisen. There was something satisfying about feeding and watering the horses, rubbing them down and brushing them, taking care of them. He'd done nearly all of it tonight, aside from successfully placating a particularly troublesome Demon.

But earlier tonight, he'd failed.

He couldn't find Mama, and he couldn't even save one woman's life. How could he be the ruler who'd protect his people? If he became lord of Rubin, would his countryside be filled with vacant farms like this?

With peasants disappearing to who-knew-where? Perhaps Weles had cursed him after all.

Everything he touched turned to ash. The people he loved were doomed to death: Roksana, Tata, Mama, and very soon, Brygida too. Even Stefan was bleeding with no signs of stopping. Every time he dared to hope, everything only came crashing down, worse than before.

He rubbed the sweat off his brow. Outside the barn doors, the sun sank below the horizon, painting the sky in pinks and purples like a fading bruise. Darkness slowly consumed the landscape.

How many more sunsets before the curse consumed Brygida?

Demon whinnied, and twin clouds of vapor escaped his nostrils. Kaspian reached for the bucket.

"Are you going to cooperate?" But he already knew the answer.

Demon stamped his foot down.

Shaking his head, Kaspian offered up the oats. Demon had won, and he buried his head in the bucket with a snort. At least someone was happy.

As night settled in, the cold was sharper, and each inhalation felt like pinpricks burning his lungs. He should head inside, but he couldn't face Brygida and Stefan and their questioning gazes. Or stand their attempts to ease his mind.

He needed a drink, but that meant getting his

saddle bag from Demon's stall. Perun's bright lightning, was the risk worth the reward? Demon *was* currently occupied with his oats.

Very slowly, he eased toward the stall door. Demon's ear flicked, but otherwise he did not lift his head from the bucket. Resting his hand on the stall door, Kaspian waited.

Demon only flicked his tail as Kaspian entered. The stall door creaked open, and Demon stamped one foot as he eased up closer.

Kaspian froze in place, ready to make a quick retreat if necessary. When Demon didn't react, he reached hesitantly for the saddle bag. Backing away slowly, he dragged it out with him.

Demon lifted his head and snuffed at Kaspian, who was already halfway out of the stall. Success.

Safe from Demon's temper, he quickly opened the saddle bag. As his hand brushed against the cold glass of the gorzałka bottle, his muscles relaxed.

Thankfully he'd brought it for a situation just like this. Just a few sips, just to take the edge off. Enough to forget the blood, and the sadness of the past couple days. Just enough to quiet the thoughts racing through his skull. That was all he needed, and then he could rejoin the others.

He took a swig, and the gorzałka burned as it ran down his throat. One swig led to another and another.

The cold didn't bother him as much, so he could stay a little longer. Just a few more minutes.

His legs weakened, and he slid down the stall wall to sit in the rotting hay.

Just a little more, and then he'd head in.

CHAPTER 17

By the light of the fire, Brygida knelt beside Stefan, unwinding the bloodstained strips of cloth from his leg, careful not to brush against his hairy thigh and keep her eyes on the gash and no higher. The tunic shirt he wore fell just below his hips, covering everything, but if he shifted wrong...

She'd never been close to a man apart from Kaspian, and they had never been *this* close. And yet she felt none of that heat pooling in her belly, or anything other than a blush that burned her face.

"You really don't have to do this," Stefan murmured.

Her eyes flickered up to his face, but he seemed to be looking everywhere but at her as she dabbed a poultice on his wound, which would keep away infection and aid healing. Thankfully Mamusia had packed some for her. "It might get infected if I don't."

He took the clean bandages and the poultice from her. "I've treated enough of my own injuries over the years. I work with Demon, for gods' sakes."

He turned his back to her, and she clasped her hands in her lap.

"Do you get hurt often, then?"

He laughed, but it lacked humor. "You could say that."

Surely the horses didn't hurt him that much? They seemed a docile lot, except for Demon, by his account. What did he do that got him injured often?

Before she could ask, he was done wrapping the wound in half the time it would have taken her. Her mouth dropped open. "Who taught you how to do that?"

His back still to her, Stefan pulled on his breeches. "My mother. She was a healer."

Was, meaning she'd passed on? What was the right thing to say in this situation? "I'm sorry to hear that. Is it just you and your father, then?"

His back tensed. "My father isn't alive anymore either." His strained tone was unlike anything she'd heard from Stefan before, as if the words burned him and pain hissed through his amiable mask.

She stood in awkward silence, not sure how to proceed. Would asking further be prying? Were his terse responses meant to draw the conversation to an end? Would she offend him if she inquired deeper?

When Stefan turned around, he was smiling once more. And dressed, praise Mokosza.

"Well, enough of my tragic tale," he said, dusting his hands off. "Where's our lordling? He's taking an awful long time feeding and watering the horses." He shook his head. "I knew I couldn't trust him to handle it. Demon probably stepped on his foot or something."

Now that he mentioned it, Kaspian had been gone a long time. "Maybe tonight's meal didn't agree with him?"

Stefan stifled a laugh and wiped at his eyes. "I shouldn't laugh, but I really, really want to." He limped toward the door and grabbed for his cloak. "I should go check on him."

"No," she replied, taking his arm. Carefully, she led him back to the bed. "I don't care how well you dress wounds, you should be resting. I'll go check on him." She placed a cup of hot tea at his bedside, along with a generous helping of rye bread, smoked grouse, and goat cheese.

"Lucky bastard," Stefan said with a grin before he helped himself to some food, his eyebrows shooting upward.

Suddenly he grimaced when he'd been just fine moments before. "I think my other leg hurts too... Maybe you should check it—"

She swatted at him, rolling her eyes.

"—just to make sure—"

"Stefan!" she scolded, laughing despite herself.

Grinning smugly, he propped himself up on the pillows, chewing his smoked grouse open mouthed. "What? A man could get used to this."

Crossing her arms, she regarded him with no amusement whatsoever.

With a heavy sigh, Stefan waved her toward the door of the cottage. "I'll be fine. Bring that lordling back here before he freezes to death. Or before Demon hammers him thin."

With one last glance to make sure Stefan had everything he needed, she slung her cloak about her shoulders, pulled up the hood, and headed outside to find Kaspian.

The waxing moon looked beautiful tonight. The sky was clear, and the stars sparkled overhead. Such a stark contrast to all the ugliness they'd seen today.

A blanket of pure snow covered the ground, and her boots crunched as she approached the open barn door. Silvery moonlight spilled onto the ground, and the horses lifted their heads in their stalls, nickering.

It was quiet. Too quiet.

"Kaspian?" she called tentatively, her voice hushed.

Her heart fluttered in her chest. This was silly. The horses seemed calm enough—if there were danger, they'd be spooked.

Nonetheless, maybe it was the looming prospect of death, but the air felt charged.

"Over here," Kaspian called, from where he sat atop a pile of hay in a dark corner of the barn.

She laughed. So he was fine. "Why are you sitting in the dark? Did the horses get the best of you?"

"I just wanted a few moments to myself." He breathed deep, resting the back of his head against a hay bale.

"Should I give you a while longer?"

He scoffed. "Don't be ridiculous." He waved her closer.

She sat beside him, her fingers brushing against his. He wrapped his warm hand around hers, and a pleasant shiver brushed over her skin.

"You look beautiful in the moonlight," he said, his breath smelling faintly of spirits. Had he been drinking? Where had he found spirits here?

But still, his touch warmed her down to her core. It always did, and tonight was no exception. She threaded her fingers with his. "So what have you been thinking about, in these few moments to yourself?"

He rolled his head to face her, his eyes soft. "What if we ran away together?"

His spirits-laden breath hit her hard, strong.

"Don't be silly." She pulled back. "We have to find your mother, and the bies, and—"

He cupped her face with one hand, his thumb caressing her cheek. A tingle raced down her spine.

"I mean after that." His hand slid to the back of her

neck, gently slipping down the hood of her cloak, drawing her even closer. "Really. Why worry about your world, my world? Let's leave them both and find another one."

His thumb rubbed the nape of her neck slowly, firmly, a rhythm she wanted to close her eyes to, feel it descend down her back, along her spine. "How are you this pretty?" He shook his head and smiled. "Have I told you that?" He leaned in closer.

Something hard pressed against her hip, painfully. An empty bottle resting against his thigh. She frowned. "Where did you find that?"

He pressed a finger to her lips. "It's nothing." He glanced toward the farmhouse and then chuckled. "Just don't tell Stefan. He doesn't like it—it reminds him of his father."

A horse nickered softly, and Kaspian traced the line of her jaw, raised her chin, and Mokosza help her, he was beautiful. Hair hued like golden wheat fields, eyes the color of the most brilliant midmorning skies. Broad shoulders and arms shaped by sword training, and hands that knew the hardness of a blade's hilt and the gentleness of a brushstroke.

She had dreamed of his mouth on hers, heat like gentle summer rays flirting with her lips, and the caress of his touch against her skin. Her mind had conjured ideas of what his body would feel like against hers, and what the sacred union of Mokosza and Perun would be like on earth. She had dreamed of it, yes, and often.

But in all her dreams, she'd never imagined the burning scent of spirits, nor the slur to his words, nor the rotting hay he'd summoned her toward. Her mind had never conjured the bottle between them, nor his growing attachment to it.

She pulled away, offering a faint smile. "We should go inside."

He returned her smile, holding her gaze, but nothing changed, nothing stirred there. As he leaned in again, her heart raced in her chest, her skin pebbling with gooseflesh. Something tightened pleasantly in her lower body, but tears welled in her eyes, cold in the winter's night.

In all her dreams, she'd never imagined that when he kissed her, it would be just a drunken man fumbling in the dark. Their every moment had been lived with such intention, and now perhaps their most important moment would become a drunken mistake?

She slipped out under his arms, but he grabbed her wrist.

"Brygida—"

She snatched her arm away, staring at the space between them with disbelieving eyes. "What are you doing?"

He shook his head, his soft gaze clearing.

"I—I'm sorry. I didn't plan on—"

"Don't," she said, holding up a hand.

"It was too soon," he said gravely, rubbing a hand over his face.

Too soon? Was that what he thought? She strode up to him. "You could have kissed me any time in the past few weeks, Kaspian. I've wanted you to. I've wished it. I've dreamed it," she said, leaning in as his mouth dropped open and his eyebrows peaked. "Any time in the past few weeks, *except* when you've been drinking."

He licked his lips and shook his head. "It's only—"

She raised her hand again. "No. You shouldn't have to get drunk to kiss me. I expect more—I demand more —than to be pawed at by a bumbling fool in the dark." She didn't wait for him to answer. "I'm going inside."

Without another word, she turned and headed back to the farmhouse.

CHAPTER 18

Brygida slept fitfully. Her dreams filled with burned cottages, bloody bodies torn to pieces, and a forest glowing with red eyes. When she woke, her skin was clammy and covered in sweat. She clutched the threadbare blanket to her chest, breath heaving as she surveyed the dark room.

On the floor, Kaspian and Stefan still slept, unaware of her nightmares. Iskra lay on Kaspian's feet, sprawled out in a pile of fluff, her paws twitching dreamily.

After what had transpired in the stable, she'd offered no more than a terse goodnight and had accepted the bed Stefan had offered her, while he and Kaspian took to the floor. She'd paged through Anita's grimoire in the swaying hearth light, attempting to make sense of the unfamiliar handwriting and mysterious shorthand.

Anita's spells to keep her slumbering witchlands calm hadn't been so different from those in the Mrok grimoire; in fact, there were a couple more. How faithfully she'd performed them, however, would remain a mystery. There was still no clear explanation for the forest's waking and her disappearance. Perhaps, more than anything, that absence had spawned her nightmares.

She clutched her vial of lake water, searching for comfort. It was a piece of home in another land, and when she closed her eyes, she could see the lake this water had come from, and not far from it, her mothers. Her breathing slowed, and she opened her eyes.

On the floor, Kaspian stirred beneath his cloak and rolled to face Stefan, snoring softly. If he hadn't been drinking last night, how differently things might have gone... Amid all the fear and danger, being together could have been a respite from it all, a moment on this journey to focus on each other, and live in that full-hearted moment.

But what should have been full hearted had been wavering. And the spirits he'd turned to for strength hurt her as much as they'd changed him. She'd fallen for Kaspian, not some spirits-numbed imitation wearing his face.

Still, as the shirt collar parted at Kaspian's neck, her fingers curled into her palm, longing to stroke the muscle there, follow it to his collarbone, and know the texture she'd find, the heat, and the way his breathing would change, and the sound he'd utter, learn the response her touch would elicit.

But maybe her fingers would never feel the truth of that longing.

Her arm throbbed then, and she rolled up her long linen sleeve. The blackmark was past her elbow now. She swallowed over the lump in her throat.

What had happened to Anita was a mystery, and it was a tragedy that a young woman had died to the wilkołaki. But for all that had happened, when it came to Lady Rubin and this blackmark, the answers didn't seem any closer. And time was running out.

Iskra's ears perked up.

There was a rap at the window.

Kaspian and Stefan slept only a few steps away. She squinted at the glass.

A black mass bobbed up and down in the predawn dimness—a *kikimora*, maybe, dissatisfied at the state of the farmhouse? When all was in order, a *kikimora* spun thread and watched over the chickens, but a disorderly house corrupted her spirit, made her malevolent and mischievous.

It tapped the window again, and Stefan's breath caught for a moment before he resumed his snoring.

She slipped out of the bed onto bare feet and tiptoed to the window. Through the blurred glass, the

Stefan slapped a palm to his forehead, but Kaspian elbowed him, already dragging on his boots.

"Let's just trust her," he said soberly. "She knows what she's doing."

Their eyes met for a moment, then his gaze descended to her feet, none too quickly. But his neutral expression hadn't changed, and he stood, fastening his coat and reaching for his cloak.

The memory of last night's almost-kiss made her cheeks blaze, but he seemed unaffected. She turned away. "You can follow me or not. But I need to see where this leads."

Without waiting for a reply, she grabbed the Scythe of the Mother and headed outside, her feet plunging knee deep into the snow. As soon as she got closer, the raven squawked and flew farther.

With a hesitant Iskra tailing them, Kaspian and Stefan did follow her despite their protests, trudging behind her as the raven hopped along in front of them.

They arrived at a clearing in the middle of the forest. Fresh snowfall blanketed the space, and the early morning light warmed it amber. Weeping willows encircled it, their branches crystallized, dangling like sparkling threads woven with iridescent beads. It was quiet all around, and the hairs at the back of her neck stood on end. At the center was a chasm, like the one near her home. A Mouth of Weles.

There was something uneasy about the place, that

set her skin crawling in the same way that the burnt cottage had made her uneasy, but this was a sacred place of worship. Its aura shouldn't have felt wrong.

The raven stopped crowing as she inched closer.

"I don't like the feel of this place." Stefan shifted from foot to foot, shivering beneath his gray cloak.

"It's a Mouth of Weles," Kaspian said to him, eyebrows drawn together.

Stefan puffed, eyeing the chasm warily. "I prefer to eat rather than be eaten, thanks." Some lighthearted humor to mask a fear of heights, maybe?

He needn't fear—they weren't going inside. Mouths of Weles opened to the world below, and she had no intention of venturing there.

She peered over the lip of the chasm, holding her scythe tightly.

A scream echoed.

She stumbled backward into a pair of waiting arms —Kaspian's. As she looked up over her shoulder, they froze, just staring at one another.

Last night, his hand had been in hers, his face so close...

Say something. But instead, she jerked away.

Why had the raven led her here? What had happened in this place?

Somehow, it had been corrupted. Its air was wrong, tainted in some way she couldn't quite place. Halina had said the demons had taken over a waking forest.

Mama and Mamusia had taught her that the witches kept the forests safe, kept the balance.

Stefan cleared his throat. "Can you ask the raven if we can leave now?"

She glared at him, but he held up his hands. How could he be joking when they'd just heard a scream?

"I mean—if you're done with your... worship?" He canted his head.

She turned on him and swept out her hand toward the Mouth of Weles. "Didn't you hear that?"

Stefan frowned. "Didn't I hear... what?"

She opened her mouth, but no words came out. When she looked to Kaspian for support, he shook his head.

"Is she all right?" Stefan whispered to him. Iskra leaned against his leg, gleaming brown eyes half closed.

Brygida whirled back toward the chasm. There had been no scream, not from there. She eyed the scythe in her hand.

It had come from the Scythe of the Mother. It had... it had *screamed*.

What happened here? she thought to its voices, but they remained silent now.

The raven hopped toward her, bobbed its head once more, and then abruptly flew away.

I give you thanks, Holy Mother, and thanks to Your messenger.

Mokosza had wanted her to know that this was

important, and she wouldn't ignore the message. But how did it fit? Weles had challenged her at a place like this. Perhaps Mokosza had moved to show Her support?

"In all seriousness," Stefan said, gently resting a hand on her forearm, "we have a long day ahead of us, I'm sure, and we should rest up before dawn. Wouldn't you agree?"

What had happened here, in this forest, at this Mouth of Weles? The gooseflesh on her arm would not recede.

"Stefan—" Kaspian began quietly.

"No, Stefan's right." She shuddered, hearing the scream in her mind anew. "Let's go."

She turned away from the chasm, but as she led the way back to the farmhouse, she couldn't shake the feeling that something or someone was watching them.

CHAPTER 19

Taking Kaspian's hand to hear the whispers of his blood had been painfully awkward, but at least they were on their way once more, having gathered their things and their horses from the abandoned farm. But the Mouth of Weles, farther and farther behind them, still lingered in her mind.

She had stowed the button in her pocket, but its wrongness burned through the fabric of her dress and the kalesony against her skin. Mokosza had bid the raven deliver it to her; she'd have to unravel its mystery.

Mamusia's dreams, the burnt cottage, the Mouth of Weles, the blackmark moving up her arm—it misted her mind like a heavy fog, its gray so thick she could see no answers. The more she thought of it all, the more distant the bies and healing the blackmark became, and she had to fight all the harder to focus on the hunt.

On her witchlands, tracking a deer in a storm, she might have doubled back as it grew colder, as the visibility worsened, as she pulled farther and farther away from the cottage. The hunt for the bies had them in the thick of many storms, but with her life and Lady Rubin's on the line, there could be no turning back. She'd have to ignore the cold, stare harder through the haze of storm winds and flurries, and quiet the foreboding racing in her chest as home fell away and away and away...

She tried to follow the whispers of Kaspian's blood, but fresh snowfall obscured any other trail they might have hoped to find. As they travelled, the wind blew stronger, piercing through her cloak and numbing her down to the bone. The relentless storm wore down the landscape's white mounds to sleek curves and crests, lifting up clouds of white powder obfuscating their way.

Through the veil, a soft amber glowed in the distance. A two-story building came into view, crusted with icicles and shrouded in snow from its foundation to its sloped roof. The letters on the signboard were too faded to decipher.

It was only too tempting to suggest stopping there, but as she adjusted her grip on the reins, her mind conjured the blackmark on her arm, right through her cloak and sleeves.

Looking into the distance, Iskra licked her nose, clearing the frost crystallizing there, and blinked inconsolably into the wind. Even with her thick fur, she needed to warm up. So did the horses. So did they all.

"This storm is getting worse." Despite the stiffness of Kaspian's mouth, his teeth clattered. "We should stop, just until it passes." His gaze met hers, a question there.

No, she did not want to stop. But if someone had to die, she'd rather it be just her to the mark later, rather than all of them freezing to death in the storm now. She nodded, but Stefan was already heading for the inn, with all the restraint of a hungry wolf descending upon a carcass.

"Praise the gods," he called back to them, and urged his horse to a canter.

Shaking her head, she followed, stifling a laugh. They made their way to a stable around the back of the inn, where a boy drank a cup of something steaming, by the smell of it tea. As soon as Stefan entered, the boy set it down and took their horses, along with some payment from Kaspian. While Stefan eagerly gathered the packs, humming a tune, they waited. His leg seemed to have recovered remarkably fast; Mama's poultice truly did work wonders.

On the boy's jacket, a pin shone, the same as the one the raven had brought her.

It had to be related to the Mouth of Weles; it bore his totem. Maybe she was wrong, but she had to check just to be certain. After all, the storm hadn't brought them here; Mokosza had.

Shaking out the snow from his hair, Kaspian looked up at her, mouth open as if he were about to say something, but in the end he lowered his gaze and joined Stefan in hefting the saddlebags. The boy watched her warily. Maybe if she paid him a compliment, he would warm to her? That seemed to be what the villagers often did. She forced a smile. "I like your pin."

He frowned and touched it, looking at her once more with a furrowed dark brow. "Do you know what it means?"

She shook her head slowly.

"It's a symbol of those who serve the Master of the World Below."

Those who served Weles? She'd known that much, given the horned serpent in its design, but who had made the pins? Distributed them? And why?

"There was a woman who lived nearby in a cottage not far from here. Do you know what happened to her?" he asked, his face serene.

His words sent a chill up her spine. Maybe it had been a mistake coming here.

She swallowed, her gaze flickering to Kaspian and Stefan in a stall nearby. "The woman in the cottage?"

He nodded, and his expression darkened.

"She was a bad person. She summoned the demonic army, so they cleansed her."

Cleansed...

The char laying claim to the interior of Anita's

cottage darkened her field of vision. *Cleansed.* The haze fell over her eyes, an ebony shroud veiling the world around her, and her blackmarked hand throbbed like a storm cloud.

The wrath of the blood coursed through her like madness, like the too-wide grin on the boy's face, the gleeful sheen to his eyes, and black whispers filtered into her ears, voices like generations layered each upon the other, upon the next and the next, darkness stretching, deepening, and soft, so quiet, quiet, speaking to her, only to her.

They cleansed her...

...cleansed her...

They. They. They.

It was them.

...cleansed. They...

The horned serpent...The horned serpent... They.

The Mouth of Weles. The Mouth...

They cleansed her...

The black whispers beckoned her to them, to keep listening, and she held out a hand for them.

Demon bucked while Stefan tried coaxing him to calmness, with Kaspian holding down a blanket that shook, violently, that trembled. A blanket that shrouded her Scythe of the Mother. It called to her hand, and her hand called back, willing it to her grasp...

"Milady?" the boy asked, canting his head, the light

of a nearby candle casting the veins of his face in stark contrast. Threads of life, like yarn, red yarn—

Her eyes frozen open, she backed away, the dark shroud clearing from her field of vision. Strong arms locked around her and swept her off her feet.

"My sister took ill in the cold, and the fever has gotten to her," Kaspian said gravely, his chest rumbling against her cheek with every word. "Is there a healer here?"

Something wet tickled her hand; Iskra licking her fingers.

"Tell my tata inside, and he'll send for her to the lord," the boy said warily. "But—"

"We'll do that!" Stefan interrupted emphatically. "Praise Weles we made it here, or there would be no hope for her." He pushed them both out the stable doors once more into the storm, bearing a satchel and a large blanket-wrapped bundle in his arms. Her Scythe of the Mother.

A relieved sigh rippled from her lips as she reached for it, but Kaspian hissed.

"Put me down," she commanded.

"No." He wouldn't even meet her eyes, simply firmed his grip on her and headed for the inn with Stefan and Iskra.

No? She opened her mouth to argue, but he hissed again. "You have a fever, remember, *sister*?" he bit out through clenched teeth.

Stefan's eyes sparked, but he looked away. Had she done something wrong?

The boy had admitted that he—or his group of mysterious "they"—had killed Anita. This village wasn't her responsibility, but Mokosza would have been honored if the Scythe of the Mother had taken the killers, every last one of *them*—those who'd murdered one of her kind.

"He didn't kill her, Brygida," Kaspian murmured as they ascended the steps.

"I didn't say he did." But he'd clearly known who had, and she would have elicited that vital information and then seen to Mokosza's justice. She rubbed her hand, soothing its ache.

It was blasphemy to say so, but would Holy Mokosza truly want her witches to suffer, to die, without fighting back? Harming a woman, even a murderer of witches, meant losing Mokosza's gifts, but why? Why would Mokosza allow the triumph of an evil woman over a good witch?

Kaspian's mouth was a grim line as they entered the inn.

The light of the interior blinded her, and she squirmed in his grip, shifting so his frost-dusted head blotted out the firelight. Warmth and the gentle hum of conversation permeated the room.

But the villagers here did not offer smiles or friendly greetings, merely narrowed eyes and suspicious stares.

There was an almost hostile tension in the air, and upon several chests, pins glinted. The horned serpent. *Them.*

Had... had these people killed Anita?

She craned her neck to get a better look, but Kaspian whirled her around. Stefan bargained with the innkeeper, a burly man with arms the size of oak trunks, and mentioned the healer—who'd find her suspiciously without fever, but now that they'd said so to the boy, they had to play to the lie.

The innkeeper assessed her with a sneer. "Your room will be ready in a few minutes, but until then, keep her away from everyone. I'll not have a malady spreading here."

With a thin smile, Stefan led the way to a small table beside the fire, where Iskra made herself immediately comfortable, and nearly as immediately—napped. Shedding their damp things, they settled in as a barmaid approached, her upper lip curled and her face locked in a grimace.

"Bring you anything?" She, too, sported a pin on her chest.

"Some beer would be—" Kaspian started to say.

"Just some *bigos* and bread for us all." Stefan cut him off, giving him a strong stare. Hunter's stew and bread only. So Stefan had had enough of Kaspian's drinking, too.

"Nothing for me. I'm not hungry." The pit of her stomach was as hard as a stone from the lake's bottom.

The barmaid gave her a long hard look before nodding curtly and leaving.

The room's balmy heat became sweltering. So many of them watched her, surrounded her, *them*. And Kaspian kept her away from them like a rabid animal, keeping the populace safe. Did he mean to protect the enemies of Mokosza?

It wasn't her duty to adjudicate them here, but... in Czarnobrzeg, if villagers donned these pins and harmed her or her mothers, would he take their side? Would he try to keep her away from them in that case, too?

The innkeeper stalked to the table, dour faced, and tossed the keys onto its surface, getting no closer. When Kaspian reached for them, she twisted from his grip.

As he tried to grab her, she snatched the keys. He began to rise, but she slammed a palm on his shoulder.

"Eat," she said, her voice colder than she'd intended, but she let it lie. She grabbed her bundled Scythe of the Mother, turned, and passed the innkeeper, headed for the rented room that matched the key.

If Kaspian wanted to, he could sit there and break bread with a room full of Mokosza's enemies. But she'd do no more than she'd come here to do. Warm up, wait for the storm to pass, and then kill a bies.

KASPIAN WATCHED HER GO, RUBBING HIS TEMPLES WITH his fingers. Should he go chasing after her, or would it only make things worse?

"I know you got drunk last night and did something to Brygida," Stefan said, spearing him with a glare from beneath dark eyebrows.

He crossed his arms and leaned forward. "What are you implying, Stef? Just say it."

Stefan shook his head but did not look away. A line etched between his eyebrows. "Your drinking has gotten out of hand. How much longer are you going to drown your feelings in spirits?"

He clutched his hands against the edge of the table, his breaths turning harsh. It wasn't *Stefan's* betrothed who'd been murdered only a few weeks ago. Not *his* father lying on his deathbed. Not *his* mother missing, in the clutches of some bies. Not the woman *Stefan* loved slowly falling victim to a demon's mark. "As long as I need to."

Stefan tilted his head, one dark eyebrow peaking. "So you 'need' to?"

Wordplay. He exhaled sharply through his nose and rolled his eyes.

"And while you 'need' to, what does that mean for everyone around you?" Stefan asked. "What if while you're so drunk you can barely walk, the bies has your mother, right in front of your face? Could you fight it?"

That wouldn't happen that way. Stefan was grasping at straws.

"What if while you're passed out drunk, your father breathes his last? And you can't even make it to his bedside?"

His gaze meandered to Stefan. This was ridiculous.

"What if last night, you'd been just a little more drunk, and ruined what you have with Brygida?"

"What do you know about that?" he shot back, then gritted his teeth.

Stefan raised his chin knowingly, but his gaze was grim as a raven's eye. "So that *is* what happened."

Huffing, he crossed his arms and shook his head. "That has nothing to do with a drink. We just had a disagreement."

"Is that what you call it?" Stefan grunted. "I'm surprised she didn't thrash you several times over, in one of many gruesome ways you don't need to imagine, because you've seen." Stefan held his gaze across the table. "You're not *you* anymore. You need help, and you won't find it at the bottom of a bottle."

Was there a person alive who could bear losing *everyone* he loved without finding some way to cope? "It's just to forget. Day and night, I am tied up in so much loss, grief, and frustration I can barely breathe.

And for a few hours here and there, I can forget, and I'm *free*, Stef."

"Forgetting isn't healing."

He had nothing to say to that and sat in silence instead, letting the ambient voices of the peasants at a nearby table and the crackle of the hearth take over.

"You're my friend, and I don't want to see you go down the path my father did. You're better than that."

Stefan's father had drunk himself to death, but worse than that, had left his marks on Stefan and had chased his mother to an early grave. He'd ruined the lives of the people he'd loved most, all to numb some old wound with spirits. He'd been a pathetic yet destructive person, threatening but tragic, and...

He could've found another way to handle his old wound. He could've faced it, instead of trying to forget it.

Kaspian rubbed his face. Stefan was right, of course. And he knew it.

But it wasn't as easy to just endure the loss. It threatened to crush him. "It's so heavy. Too heavy. What am I supposed to do?"

A gentle smile tugged at Stefan's mouth, an expression he'd rarely seen, and Stefan opened his arms. "Come to me. To Brygida. To any of us who care about you. And talk. Keep talking until all the words twisting inside come out, and don't stop coming back and talking until it's not too heavy anymore."

He pressed his lips tight, swallowed. It wasn't easy to just go to someone and... talk. Stefan, Brygida, everyone had their own lives, things to do, and wouldn't have time to just listen to him whine and lament until he felt better. Besides, men didn't rely on others to keep them strong. What if it changed how they saw him?

But then... not turning to others for support had produced men like Stefan's father.

"And give yourself something else to do." A half-laugh escaped Stefan. "Tell me, why don't I find paintings stashed in my stable anymore?"

When he painted, his hands always found their way back to one subject: Roksana. It had hurt, time and again, to try to express her on the canvas, to attempt it in vain, and he'd... retreated from it. From her. But there was something in his heart that needed to be said, that could only be spoken in oils and brushstrokes. Maybe he needed to let it speak.

A woman cleared her throat—the barmaid. Tears welled in her eyes as she set down the bread and bigos, sniffling and wiping at her cheek. She gave Stefan a radiant smile, nodded, and left them to it. And Perun's bright lightning, did Stefan watch her go.

At least it saved him from having to reply. He avoided Stefan's stare by soaking the nearly stale bread in the bigos, pushing the fermented cabbage and various meats around.

The table next to them got up abruptly and left.

He looked up. The tavern had cleared out; only a few peasants remained.

"Something isn't right." Stefan reached for the blade at his hip. Iskra's head perked up, and with her tail down, she crept to stand behind them.

The few remaining men stood.

It was all coming back—the mob, the glint of Agata's blade—

No. Not again.

He reached for his sword.

The peasants closed in, and his chest constricted. One man grabbed for Stefan, who swung a punch and knocked him back a few steps.

"Kaspian, move!" Stefan shouted.

He drew his sword and leveled it at the peasants who came near him. What were they, compared to the wilkołaki?

But they drew no weapons.

Perun's bright lightning, had they attacked Brygida? Had they caught her sleeping?

He pushed up against the two men blocking his path, shoved one and hit the other in the nose with his sword's pommel. They grabbed his arms as he tried to pull toward the inn's rooms. "Brygida!"

Stefan shouldered past the men in front of him, making a path toward the inn's front door, but the others blocked his way. "We don't want any trouble here! Just let us and our friends leave," Stefan shouted at them.

Iskra barked at the strangers, backing up and whining.

The door blew open and, with it, the howling wind and a flurry of snow.

A tall, black-cloaked man entered, surrounded by armored guards.

Brygida ran into the main room, her scythe in hand, gaze snapping from him to Stefan to the door.

"I'm afraid none of you are leaving," said Lord Granat, removing his hood.

CHAPTER 20

Brygida grasped her vial, ready to unleash the wrath of the blood if necessary. But Lord Granat's guards didn't draw any weapons nor move to attack them.

No, not guards...

Beside him stood two younger people, a man and a woman, both with the same ash-blond hair and dark-brown eyes. The same eyes Lord Granat had. Were they his children?

The man was handsome, with a sculpted jaw and sharp cheekbones, a frame as tall and broad as Kaspian's but brawnier, like that of a seasoned warrior. A couple of scars at his brow and the periphery of his face marred his beauty, but lent him an intimidating air. The woman's figure wasn't much different—she'd outmatch even Halina in a test of strength—but she had a heart-shaped face, with flinty, cold eyes that belied any soft-ness to her features. Just as intimidating as her probable brother.

"What do you want from us?" Kaspian bit out, hand reaching for his sword.

"I need you to come with me." There was nothing malicious in Lord Granat's expression; it was blank. And when she'd met him at Kolęda, he had seemed kind, one of the few people there who hadn't looked at her with horror and fear.

Villagers around the room watched them with wary gazes. A whisper of warning snaked from the scythe.

"I'll come with you, but leave them out of it." Kaspian gestured to Brygida and Stefan.

"It's the witch we need, not you," Lord Granat's daughter snapped.

The *witch*. Their lie to the innkeeper had just crumbled.

"Silence your tongue, Urszula," Lord Granat said to the woman, glancing around the room at the restless villagers.

The barmaid slipped out a back door. Lord Granat's daughter, Urszula, lowered her head as if chastised.

But the damage was already done. The villagers stood, closing in around them.

The fevered whisper from the scythe grew in inten-sity, like a buzzing in her ears, and she grasped her vial of lake water tighter. The burning gaze of the villagers was enough to set her aflame. There was madness in those eyes, the same sort of serene malice that had lingered in the stable boy's gaze.

Kaspian put an arm out to shield her from Lord Granat as Stefan drew his dagger, facing the growing mob. She placed a hand on Kaspian's shoulder, and he tensed.

"I think we should go with him." Now that the villagers knew she was a witch, they couldn't stay here.

Kaspian's lips pressed into a thin line. "Are you sure?"

She bit her lip and nodded. Whatever reason had brought Lord Granat here, she didn't think he wished her harm.

"We'll come with you." Kaspian said the words, but his bitter tone expressed just how unhappy he was about it.

Lord Granat and his children led the way out of the inn, while the crowd of villagers took up the rear, facing Stefan, who covered her back. Surrounded like this, her entire body was tense. Nothing in nature cared to be backed into a corner. But if she didn't go with Lord Granat, there was no telling what she'd face here, and who would be hurt.

As she stepped out of the inn, the barmaid leaped into her path, her face twisted. "Death to witches!"

The barmaid flung a powder toward her.

Kaspian pushed her out of the way. She landed hard in the snow.

He shouted, clutching at his eyes, rubbing at his face. No. Was he—

Urszula punched the barmaid in the face, sending her flying. "You dare?" she yelled. "In the presence of your lord?"

Kaspian—

The villagers closed in around them.

Before she could react, Urszula grabbed her by the arm and dragged her away.

Kaspian knelt in the snow, hands over his eyes, doubled over while Stefan and Lord Granat's son pushed back the crowd.

Brygida yanked her arm away from Urszula and rushed to Kaspian's side, her entire body trembling. She ran assessing hands over him, but he seemed uninjured. "Come, take my shoulder. We have to get out of here."

"Brygida—" he stammered, rubbing his eyes. "I... I think I'm blind."

❧

BRYGIDA WRUNG HER HANDS TOGETHER AS LORD Granat's healer examined Kaspian's face in the quiet of a Grobowski manor guest chamber. His eyes were swollen shut, and the skin around them was red.

As the healer gently pressed against the inflamed skin, Kaspian suppressed a groan, and every probe pricked as if it were her own flesh. Whatever it was that barmaid had thrown at him, it had been meant for her.

The healer put a salve on his skin before wrapping a cloth around his eyes with a shake of her head.

"Why can't I see?" Kaspian asked, his voice barely above a murmur.

"It's difficult to say," the old healer replied. "I suspect they used hogsweed, which grows abundant here and when concentrated and applied to the eyes, can cause inflammation. The swelling could be affecting your sight, and you might regain it once the swelling goes down. Or you might never recover. Only time will tell."

Never...?

Kaspian pressed his lips together, his hands clasped over his abdomen on the bed. He hadn't moved since they'd arrived, and even now, he didn't even shift. To get this grim outlook... He had to be coming undone, but was he putting on a brave face for her sake?

"He'll need to keep applying this salve." The healer handed Brygida a small pot. "And keep his bandages clean."

She nodded, feeling empty inside. Lightly touching her shoulder, the healer left the chamber and shut the door quietly, leaving them alone.

For a few moments, they sat in silence. What could

she say to him when he'd put his life on the line for her, had potentially lost his sight because of her?

Tears beaded on her lashes and rolled down her cheek. She took a seat on the bed beside him, covering his clasped hands with her palm. He brushed her hand with his fingers.

For him to never see again because he'd tried to save her was unfair. That poison had been meant for her, and the gods would be too cruel to take the sight of a painter away.

"Even if I never see again, I wouldn't change what I did."

A sob escaped her throat as she wrapped her arms around his neck, feeling the beating of his heart as his strong arms encircled her.

"Don't cry. The healer did say there's a chance it's not permanent."

She rubbed her tears away with the back of her hand. He was right. It might not be permanent, but even so, he had risked everything for her.

There was a knock at the door, and she started just as a maid popped her head in. "Lord Granat requests that you join him and his family presently for dinner."

Brygida nodded.

"Thank you," Kaspian said, turning toward the maid, who bowed and shut the door.

In the ensuing silence, he stroked her hand, the blackmarked one, as if it were a treasure. As if it weren't attached to the reason he couldn't see. Holding her wrist up to her mouth, she bit back tears. He'd asked her not to cry.

And in that moment he'd fallen to his knees in the snow, she'd realized that for his sake, her heart knew no bounds. Not crying was only the beginning, and the rest... The rest she'd have him know, as clearly and as deeply as this fleeting body of hers could manage.

CHAPTER 21

The bed shifted beneath Kaspian as Brygida moved, still holding his hand. Two soft footfalls creaked on the floor, and she urged him to rise. He wanted to thank her for leading him to the dining hall, or perhaps joke that he'd never been great with directions, but everything he wanted to say only felt like it would make her feel worse. And that was the last thing he wanted.

He followed her lead, rising from the bed, and let her guide him by the hand wherever she wanted. Slowly, she led him to where the servant's voice had come from, and then, abruptly, she whirled him around and pushed him lightly, until his back met the wall. No, it clicked—the door.

He huffed a laugh. If she walked him right into a door, then perhaps her mood had lightened after all?

But a touch pressed against his chest, and another, fingertips and palms resting against him gently. "Brygida?" he asked quietly, but he didn't move.

Those fingertips stroked from his chest and up his neck, over his jaw to clasp both sides of his face, which went pleasantly taut beneath her touch. Softness rested flush against him as she leaned her body against his, then smoothed it upward as she rose and drew his mouth down to hers.

Her lips brushed against his, soft and supple, teasing his mouth with the slowest, gentlest whisper of contact. Her quiet breaths warmed his skin, making him shiver as her lips met his once more, a little firmer this time.

His hands found her hips, but he schooled them, suppressing their every desire to wander further, to wrap her tight, to never let go. She leaned into him, her teeth just grazing his bottom lip as her mouth broke away from his, but she remained there a moment, just breathing deep breaths. Each one rose and fell against his own chest, shared the same air, and what he wouldn't give to see her expression right now, to be able to savor this aureate moment.

Then she slowly pulled away, her hand drawing his toward her. He made no attempt to gather his composure—he was fairly certain it wasn't possible—and lumbered in the direction she urged.

A creak broke the silence, the door opening, and she

navigated him into the corridor adeptly.

As Brygida led him through the manor house, so many words formed in his mind only to dissipate into ether before he could say them. Sometimes too many elements ruined the composition, and although he couldn't see, this one felt perfect without a single thing more.

Even though it had been brief, the touch of her lips against his had left a lasting impression. But as it was, he was trapped in darkness in enemy territory, with only her lead to guide him.

His sight might never return, and dinner was the last thing on his mind right now. There was no way he could shove even a single spoonful of food into his mouth, but he had to know what Lord Granat wanted with Brygida, why he'd brought them here and had his healer treat his wounds.

Brygida halted her steps, and Kaspian stopped behind her. A chair scraped against the floor.

"Please, join us," Lord Granat's voice rumbled.

An ember popped. Someone close by cleared his throat and cloths shuffled. Kaspian swiveled his head around, trying to gain his bearings in the unfamiliar surroundings.

Brygida tugged him gently, guiding his hand to a polished wooden chair back, and then assisted him in sitting.

"What did the healer say?" Stefan's voice was near,

and Kaspian jerked in the direction of the sound.

"It's likely temporary blindness," he said in the direction he thought Stefan would be.

Stefan exhaled. "Perun be praised."

"I am sorry for your injuries," Lord Granat said from somewhere to Kaspian's left. "My healer is at your disposal until you've recovered enough to travel home, of course."

The table vibrated with a thud. "The audacity of them to attack a guest in the presence of their lord."

Urszula's furious voice. She must've struck the table with a fist.

Everything he'd been told about Lord Granat was that he was a merciless tyrant, who ruled his region beneath an iron fist. And yet these peasants had thrown poison at Brygida right in front of their own lord. It made no sense.

"Sister." A low murmur across the table from Kaspian.

"Don't try and silence me, Nikodem. I've held my tongue long enough, and look where it's gotten us. The entire region has gone mad!" Her voice rose as something clinked like a glass being knocked over.

There was a shuffle of cloth and hurried footsteps.

"I take it this attack wasn't the first?" Stefan asked cautiously.

"No. Unfortunately, it is not," Lord Granat replied.

Footsteps approached from Kaspian's right, and he

jerked his head and elbow backward, hitting something soft and fleshy.

A gentle hand on his shoulder.

"She's brought you soup," Brygida said softly in his ear.

Kaspian swallowed down his embarrassment. "My apologies."

The loss of his sight put him on edge. Everything was an unknown.

The scent of food and the warmth of steam wafted over his face. Even if he'd wanted to eat, the idea of fumbling with a spoon right now, in front of Lord Granat and his children, was not appealing. He looked in what he hoped was Lord Granat's direction. "What does all of this have to do with Brygida?"

"You should show some respect," Urszula grumbled.

It was strange, coming from her. Her outburst at the inn had given that barmaid motive to attack Brygida.

And this was the woman his mother would have him marry? She'd more likely eviscerate him before she'd wed him.

"Forgive me. Thank you for coming to our aid," he said, doing his very best to keep the sarcasm from his voice. But for Lord Granat's arrival, they might've been able to leave the inn unscathed.

Urszula scoffed.

"Be silent," Lord Granat gritted out to his daughter. "Or you will leave this table."

An uncomfortable quiet answered, until Lord Granat cleared his throat. "Demons have been roaming through our region, sowing discord among the peasantry. It started out with a few isolated incidents. A sighting, then a death. But with each passing week, the problem grows worse. More and more have been turning to the Cult of Weles and their wicked practices." There was something in Lord Granat's voice that made the hairs on the back of his neck stand on end.

"Are they the ones that have been killing the witches?" There was an edge to Brygida's voice, the same edge when she'd seen that stable boy's smug grin.

Under the table, he fumbled to take her hand, then squeezed it. She didn't squeeze back.

"They have, which has only made the problem worse," Lord Granat replied.

Brygida pulled her hand away from his.

"Why would I want to help murderers?" Brygida asked icily, so unlike her.

"What difference does it make? People are dying, and your kind are supposed to protect against things like this demon, aren't you?" Urszula's voice spiked higher.

Feet shuffled, and something clattered on the ground. Stefan grabbed Kaspian by the shoulder as if to pull him back. Kaspian swung his head back and forth.

"Enough," Lord Granat's voice boomed.

There was a long, strained silence. Perun's bright

lightning, if only he knew what was happening here.

"What's going on?" he asked.

"Brygida and Urszula are about turn over this table," Stefan whispered in his ear.

A cold dread sank through him. He never should have brought Brygida here.

"Innocent people are being turned into demons, good people who respected the witches," Nikodem murmured, his voice low.

Innocent people were being turned? Perhaps the wilkołaki hadn't all been—

"I told you we couldn't trust her," Urszula said.

"Why me?" Brygida's voice, hardened, sounded ready for battle. "Why not go to the Huntresses of Dziewanna? They have immunity."

"They pride themselves on their kills," Lord Granat answered, as if that were a disadvantage. "We do need the demons dealt with, but one in particular... It... it needs to survive. You see, Lady Rubin is one of those who were turned."

Not Mama. Had she been one of the wilkołaki?

His head spun, and he braced against the table.

"You're lying." He tried to stand but knocked over the bowl on the table. Hot soup burned his hand and soaked his sleeve, and he hissed. Light footsteps rushed toward him, and gentle hands dabbed at his arm. Brygida's.

"I wish it weren't true," Lord Granat said quietly.

"But I saw it with my own eyes. Lady Rubin and I went into the forest together. On our way, the demon attacked and we were separated. By the time I found her again, it was too late. She'd already started to turn and fled from me."

"Why would she even go to the forest?" And with Lord Granat of all people? Kaspian's chest tightened, and the floor swayed beneath him.

Stefan put an arm around him to steady him.

"She was seeking Brygida. She wanted to ask her to end her relationship with you. The villagers would never accept a witch as the future lady of Rubin. She and I had discussed it at length, and we both agreed that my daughter, with her skill in leadership, would help you effectively rule Rubin. Her prowess with a blade and knack for leadership would balance you, we felt."

Just like that. So matter-of-factly.

Mama's scheming and politicking had led to her own undoing, and he wanted to be angry at her; he did. He'd finally found someone he loved, someone who made him happy, and all Mama had done had been to try thwarting that love, that happiness, at every turn.

But Lord Granat knew her well. No, *Oskar*, as she'd called him. He knew her beliefs, her feelings, her. He cared, at least enough to go to all this trouble. And that moment he'd spied the two of them... He didn't need to be told anymore what it was, because he'd felt it. Love.

Mama loved Oskar. She loved him, but she was married to Tata. She was lady of Rubin. She'd put the people and the region first. The rulership.

And those had always been her priorities. She didn't approve of Brygida, but it was more than that. He'd seen it here in Granat; the villagers had turned on the witches. They'd never accept Brygida, and deep down, he'd always known that. Even Stryjek Andrzej had tried to tell him what would happen if he continued to side with the witches. It wasn't their fault, and they weren't the enemies of the village or his family. But Mama had known that while he chased Brygida, there would never be stability. He'd courted Brygida openly, recklessly, endangering both their lives, their families, everything.

And because he'd been blind to it, Mama had been turned into a bies and Brygida had been blackmarked. Both of their lives now hung in the balance.

Had he been willing to talk to Mama, to just listen and perhaps find an alternate way forward for all of them, would any of this have happened? Was all of this *his* fault?

"Do you know where the demon is?" Brygida asked, cutting the silence.

"I do. I've been tracking it for some time," Urszula answered. "Will you help?"

Brygida pulled away from him, the fabric of her dress swishing as she rose. "Take me to it."

CHAPTER 22

T he blackmark covered Brygida's entire arm, cloaking her elbow and stretching tendrils across her chest toward her heart. There was no more time to delay. The demon that Lord Granat and his family had tracked had to be the right one. The skin on her arm was tight, and she rolled her stiff shoulder as she joined the others in the courtyard.

"She's my mother," Kaspian said firmly to Urszula. "I'm coming."

"You'll only get in the way." She waved him off dismissively.

"My mother was turned by this demon because of me. I'll not abandon her because it's more convenient for you," he hissed back.

No one had a greater stake in finding the bies than

she and Kaspian. There was no way she would allow Urszula to dictate their involvement.

Urszula claimed he'd only get in the way, but the fact was, none of them knew with any certainty how to fight it when it could take control of anyone. When she'd gotten close last time, its hold over her had been too strong; if not for Halina, she might have ended up just like Lady Rubin.

They didn't have a plan, but they also had no choice. At least she didn't, with the blackmark so close to taking her life.

As Urszula stormed off, Brygida put her hand on Kaspian's shoulder. He flinched, angling his hand in her direction, his eyebrows drawing together over his blindfold.

"It's me," she whispered to him.

"Brygida." He smiled wistfully.

That kiss they'd had, that perfect kiss, almost made her want to weep. To know its sweetness, its pleasure, and then to die the next day? It was too cruel. There had to be a way to defeat the bies.

She took his hand in both of hers, idly stroking his fingers. "I have to fight the bies, Kaspian. If I don't, I won't see the dawn. I can feel it."

He squared his shoulders. "I know that. We'll make it in time."

She shook her head. "What I mean is, if I fail, you

might be able to learn something from my attempt, petition the Huntresses of Dziewanna to help you."

He went rigid, but then he turned to face her. "Brygida, I won't pretend I'll be useful to you in this fight, but I'd rather die where I stand than leave you to face it alone." His hand reached toward her hair, then he tucked a tendril behind her ear. "I know there are a dozen reasons why we can't have a future together, and I won't rest until I see each and every one defeated. Including this one."

When he made such promises to her, it only encouraged her lips to meet his anew. She rose to press a kiss to his mouth, and he embraced her. "Together, then."

He nodded.

I will protect you, she pledged. She didn't know how, not yet, but she wouldn't lose Kaspian to the bies if it was the last thing she did.

Guiding him by the hand, she led him to their horses, and they mounted up. Kaspian's hand in hers, she listened to the hum of his blood.

She had to strain to distinguish the ties, but one was closer than the others. "This way."

Together with Urszula, Nikodem, Lord Granat, Stefan, and a complement of guards, she and Kaspian headed out into the woods.

Ice crunched under hooves as they picked their way through the waking forest once more, and the offering to the błędnica must have worked, since it kept the lesser demons at bay.

Brygida took Kaspian's hand again and again, trying to concentrate on his blood tie, but the direction kept changing. The wind howled through the trees, and she shifted in her seat, staring in all directions.

"Do you know where you're going?" Urszula demanded, then looked to her brother for support; he merely lowered his gaze.

"We're very close, but it's on the move and we're two steps behind." Straining once more, she tried to follow the blood tie's direction.

Snow hit the ground, and above, a bough wavered beneath a raven's weight.

"Look who's back," Stefan said, more brightly than she'd expected.

Mokosza's messenger. It had led her to the Mouth of Weles before, and perhaps it could now lead them to the bies.

It squawked at her before fluttering ahead.

She urged Demon forward, chasing after the raven among the unfamiliar trees, the hoofbeats of the other horses following after her.

Then a flap of wings, and the raven disappeared.

She slowed, letting Demon take her down a narrow path amid densely packed trees. The forest fell silent, with neither animal calls nor howling winds disturbing the eerie quiet. Darkness clung to the shadows, and the cold bit deeper. Above her, the sky turned black, but as she squinted—

Ravens crowded the canopy, dozens of them, perched on every available branch, a dark swath stretching straight ahead to a clearing. Watching them, she proceeded carefully, until they opened their black beaks and shrieked like bats.

An otherworldly howl rent the air, so loud it reverberated inside her body.

She gripped the Scythe of the Mother. All the ravens abandoned their perches, a myriad of black wings blotting out everything.

Demon jolted out of the way.

Dark feathers parted for the glow of red eyes, set in a massive body dripping with shadows.

Nikodem caught up to her, his horse rearing as huge jaws clamped down on its neck. Blood spattered the snow while the animal screamed, and Nikodem leaped from the saddle. With a swipe of enormous claws, bark and splinters shot from breaking trees.

Brygida dismounted, willing the scythe to call forth its crystalline ice blade.

"Fan out!" Urszula shouted as the rest of the group closed in.

The bies, however, was more preoccupied with devouring the steaming remains of the dead horse. The way it behaved was so different than how it had before, and perhaps it was a bit smaller, its quills of dark fur slightly shorter.

Could this be—?

With Stefan's help, Kaspian climbed down from the saddle, and then he very slowly approached the bies.

It lifted its head, red eyes taking in the people around it, not narrowing on any one person. It swayed uncertainly, exposing pointed teeth to Kaspian as he got closer. Across from her, Urszula held a fist in the air while the guards accompanying them drew their bows and waited.

A whisper tickled at Brygida's ear, and her black-marked arm burned. The bies had its eyes locked on Kaspian now and moved closer.

But something wasn't right. It raised its beastly head and turned away from Kaspian.

A second growl ripped through the air, shaking the ground. Another bies barreled into the clearing.

Urszula lowered her fist and arrows flew.

...*see into you*...

Don't look, don't look, don't look...

...*fear His power*...

The scythe's innumerable voices layered over one another chaotically.

For a moment, Urszula locked eyes with the second bies and froze.

Was that how it gained control of minds?

"Avert your eyes from its gaze!" Brygida shouted,

drawing upon the wrath of the blood to take hold of the deep snow.

The bies charged through the line of guards, scattering them in all directions. Once it was clear of them, she could attack.

It skidded through the snow, straight for her.

She leaped from its path, but for a moment, for just a moment, she met its eyes.

The whispering in her dominated, its slick fingers burying deeper into her mind as her entire arm throbbed, radiating with shackled lightning. The dark haze fell over her field of vision, like looking through a black shroud.

Until someone shoved her face down toward the snow.

"Cover your eyes," Nikodem said, then sprang to his feet, his sword drawn.

"Over here," Kaspian shouted. Knees bent, he faced the second bies, his arms out wide. Blindfolded and unable to see, he wouldn't fall prey to the bies's mind control.

She wavered, hoping the bies would heed Kaspian, and yet hoping it would ignore him, leave him be—

It changed course, heading straight for him.

Keeping her gaze low to the ground, she pulled the snow to her command, summoned the waters from all around her, raising ice spikes that raced toward the bies.

It turned on her, but she wouldn't meet its eyes.

Dark ichor pelted the ground as the ice spikes struck its lower body.

Her hand burned, all the way up her arm and to her chest, and the whispers inside her head screeched.

She clutched at her agonized temples, struggling to stay on her feet, leaning on the scythe for support. The bies didn't need eye contact, not from her, not when the blackmark linked them inextricably.

... are you?

Who you are...

...who are...

The chaos of the scythe's quiet voices cut in.

The screeching hit a higher pitch, sending a wave of pain cracking through her mind. The burnt cottage, the Mouth of Weles, the scream of a witch plummeting to her death. It forced her to her knees, the never-ending clash of two worlds pulling at the two ends of her being.

A place where she didn't belong.

The deaths of witches who'd tried.

Kaspian blinded for her sake.

The crack widened and widened, opening a path for the shadows between, the shadows that would darken, that would never stop until they claimed everything. She clung to both sides, willing them back together, but the gap only expanded. The harder she tried to hold both ends together, the closer she was to ripping apart.

There was only one way to save herself, to stop the

bies, to save them all. Letting go of what stretched her over the abyss. Taking a side.

Through the screech of invading voices, she grasped her vial of lake water and screamed. "I am a Mrok witch!"

Her limbs shook as the power flowed through her, filling her to nearly overflowing. The snow melted to rise around her like a whirlpool, churning around and around. As the bies lurched toward her, the whirlpool froze outward into deadly spikes.

One impaled the bies lunging for her, right through its center mass, and another followed. And another.

With one final thrust of her power, she yanked the spikes outward in all directions, blasting the bies to pieces. As the ice hit the trees, it melted to water, flowing down the bark in frosty rivulets.

The bies collapsed into the snow, and she held its gaze as the burning embers of its shadowy face began to fade.

A thousand needles poked through her black-marked arm, and she screamed. Darkness seeped from her chest, shoulder, and arm like smoke, tendrils flowing toward the bies's dying body, only to dissipate. It flowed and flowed and flowed, needling out of her until only a black crescent remained on her palm.

She'd done it. She'd defeated the bies and passed Weles's challenge.

She blinked at the mark sluggishly, tumbling to hands and knees in the snow.

The guards crowded in to examine the bies's body.

The second bies fell into the snow behind it, crumpled like a dying spider.

CHAPTER 23

Kaspian swiveled his head around as voices overlapped one another. The world was still cast in blurry shadows, but from what he'd gathered, Brygida had defeated the bies. A metallic stench clung to the air.

Arms outstretched, he stumbled toward the direction of the voices.

"The monster is transforming!" an unfamiliar voice shouted from behind him.

He spun toward it. "What's going on? Stefan? Brygida?" He held out his hand, desperate for someone to take it, to guide him. A strong forearm met his palm.

"It's Lady Rubin," Stefan said before clearing his throat, "and she's, um, naked..."

Mama, alive? His heart lightened as he clutched Stefan's sleeve. "Where is she? Bring me to her, please."

"Sabina!" Oskar bellowed, and fast, heavy boot steps followed.

He began to move in their direction when a cold hand grasped his.

"I'll take you." Brygida's voice. Along with Stefan, she led him to where all the voices had congregated. So many spoke, but he hadn't yet heard Mama's voice. Something was wrong.

"Is she hurt?"

"She's unconscious but breathing," Oskar's voice answered, uncharacteristically soft, almost tender. They truly did love each other, didn't they?

"Let's return to the manor," Lord Granat added, his tone more authoritative this time. He grunted with a burst of effort, perhaps hefting up Mama.

"Wait," Brygida entreated heartfully. "Please." Her hand raised his, and then his fingers met the smooth skin of another hand. Mama's.

Perun's bright lightning, she was *warm*. She was *alive*.

His blindfold moistened and his useless eyes burned, but none of that mattered. Mama was alive.

As they headed away, toward the whinnies of horses, he couldn't let her go. It still didn't feel real somehow, even with her hand in his, and maybe it wouldn't until he saw her with his own eyes, or heard her voice.

Stefan guided him back into the saddle, and Oskar

helped place Mama before him, wrapped in a heavy woolen and furred cloak. He held her securely, unconcerned with riding since Stefan bore his mount's reins.

Oskar ordered his son and some guards to stay behind and burn the bies, and then they hurried back to the manor. The entire way, he listened for some sign of change in her breathing, for her voice to speak up, but she remained unchanged the whole ride back. Hopefully it was just exhaustion; it would be miraculous if a person could be a demon for nearly a week unscathed.

When they came to a stop, careful arms took Mama from him, but he held her hand as they took her inside and upstairs. Someone seated him in a bedside chair and then many footsteps and voices coordinated to rest Mama on the bed. They took care of her as the healer's gnarled voice murmured to herself. Claw-tipped paws clicked into the room, and Iskra's panting and whimpering punctuated the healer's words.

A sharp smell, some medicinal herb perhaps, and a low groan came from the bed.

"Mama? Are you awake?"

Fabric swished as she shifted, and a hand squeezed his. "Kaspian...?" Her fingers traced over his cheek and then withdrew. "What's happened to you?"

He shook his head. "It doesn't matter now that you're safe." He grasped, fumbling for her shoulder, and pulled her into his tight embrace.

She stroked his back in slow circles just as she had when he was a boy. He hadn't realized how much he'd missed that touch, missed her, while the distance had grown between them. It had taken nearly losing her to make him realize it. With a happy bark, Iskra jumped onto the bed, giving Mama a jolt before she gasped.

They pulled apart, and by Iskra's excited breaths, she could only be getting her long-awaited pets from Mama.

"My son, tell me. Please. What happened to you?" She cupped his cheek as her voice quivered.

"An attack on the road," he answered. "Don't worry. My vision is already improving." He could see vague blurs and shadows after all, and there was no sense in distressing her now. "What about you? Are you hurting anywhere?"

"I'm fine, but... where are we?" The bed depressed as she moved.

He didn't want to shock her too quickly. "Do you remember what happened?"

A few frustrated breaths. "All I remember is going into the forest, and then that... *thing* attacked..." There was a long pause. "I... I remember..." She gasped again, a choked sound.

He took her hand and squeezed. "It wasn't your fault, what you did while you were transformed. You weren't yourself."

A quiet sob. "I never should have gone into those

woods. I was so angry after we fought, and I thought if I could only convince the witch to leave you be..."

Kaspian flinched at those words. It was likely Mama would never see Brygida as a good match for him, no matter how hard he tried. But he didn't want to argue anymore. After all was said and done, she was his mother and he'd nearly lost her once. And he didn't want their differences to come between them anymore. "I said some awful things to you. Your anger was justified, and I'm sorry."

She stroked his hand lovingly. "What I wanted to say to you that day when we argued was... I knew you were upset that we didn't believe you were innocent. But what I need you to understand is that—and Perun help me"—she took a deep breath—"guilty or not, it didn't matter. I wanted to believe that if you'd done wrong, I'd let you take responsibility for your actions, but whether you're innocent or guilty, good or bad, you're my son. I had to protect you. I couldn't stand by and let you die. And that day I went with your father to the witches' cabin, that was all I wanted. For you to live. You'll understand this when you have children of your own, but I love you far more than anything you can understand. Far more than anyone else in this world, far more than justice, far more than responsibility. And I always will." She squeezed his hand again.

All this time he'd been clinging onto this hurt and resentment for what she had done. But if he had only just stopped and let her explain herself, then they could have grieved together for Roksana... and soon for Tata. He embraced her again. "I'm sorry. I condemned you for doubting me while never giving you a chance to explain yourself."

She stroked the top of his head. "You are my son, and no matter what, I will always love you."

"I promise, I will try to do better from now on."

Mama wrapped his arms around his shoulders, pulling him tight. And he meant it—no matter what it took, he would make sure he did better by her and Tata.

There was a knock at the door. Kaspian squinted toward it but could see nothing beyond dark shadows.

"Come in," Mama said.

The door creaked as it opened. Heavy footsteps and a hulking form approached. "I'm sorry to intrude."

A little gasp. "Not at all, Oskar. My son and I are thankful for your hospitality." It was the same tender voice she'd used with him on Kolęda. This wasn't about politics; Oskar would've benefited far more from Kaspian's death and Mama never returning. What they had was true, as problematic as that was for his parents' marriage. He still didn't understand what it all meant.

"You are always welcome in my home, Sabina." Oskar's tone softened as well.

"Thank you, Lord Granat, for everything," Kaspian said, trying to cut the awkward tension in the room.

"It is I who should be grateful to you. You've done a

great service to my region. I... wish I had better news to share."

Kaspian's stomach clenched. *No. Please not Tata.* Ewa had said he had a week, and surely a couple days remained?

But in all the chaos, he'd lost track of time. What if Tata was gone?

"What is it?" Mama asked, her voice breaking. Did she fear the same?

"One of your subjects, a man named Dariusz Baran, reached out to me some time ago as he has been doing for weeks, offering to give me information about Rubin for a price."

Then it was as Nina had said. Dariusz was a traitor.

Oskar cleared his throat. "I received word that the peasants are planning to attack the witches. They believe the witches are responsible for your disappearance, Sabina, and Lord Rubin's declining health."

Kaspian stood up and collided with the bed on his way to get out the door.

"Kaspian, what are you doing?" Mama called.

He needed the gods' own speed. "I have to warn Brygida. Her mothers are in danger."

A firm hand fell on his shoulder. "I will not send you alone. Urszula and Nikodem shall accompany you. You've helped my region, and I will help you protect yours. We cannot let this Cult of Weles grab a stronger foothold in Nizina."

Kaspian looked in the direction of Oskar's voice. "I thank you. I will not forget this, but I have to tell Brygida."

"She's already been informed and is preparing to leave."

His taut shoulders relaxed, if only a little.

Mama squeezed his hand. "Let's go home."

Home. It seemed like an eternity since he'd been in Czarnobrzeg. Hopefully he'd arrive in time, for Tata's sake and for Brygida's mothers.

CHAPTER 24

B rygida led the ride back to her witchlands, her heart in her throat as Demon flew over the countryside. Mama and Mamusia were in danger, and even with the snow melting some, they couldn't get there fast enough.

They moved as quickly as they could without hurting the horses, but every moment that passed, the mob of villagers could be getting closer to the cottage, to her mothers inside and unaware of what awaited them. Following the road rather than a meandering trail dictated by a blood tie, they made better time, but it took riding day and night, past the exhaustion, past the complaints, and changing horses at two small villages to make it to Rubin in two days' time.

She'd barely slept, taking only a couple hours when they were forced to stop, but Kaspian and Lady Rubin looked even worse for wear. Lady Rubin was still regaining her strength and Kaspian's sight still hadn't returned, but they'd done everything to save his mother. Now it was time to do that for both of hers.

At last, Czarnobrzeg's manor house and the small cluster of village buildings was in sight. The Perun-struck oak's bare limbs reached for the sky, as if to beckon her home.

But as they approached, a group on horseback rode toward them from the distance. Their whole cavalcade drew to a halt to meet them.

The men on horseback wore Rubin's white-and-red tabards and carried swords at their hips. Guards. But she reached for the vial of lake water, just in case.

"Master Kaspian, Lady Rubin, we're glad you've returned," said the man at the front of the group, as he bowed his head to them.

"My father?" Kaspian asked.

The man shook his head. "Not well. The healer does not expect him to make it to the end of the day. The village has been rising up because they are certain it's a witch's curse that struck him ill. We've done our best to keep them from acting out, but a big group is making its way to the Madwood."

There was no time. "We have to hurry," she said to Kaspian, urging her horse toward her witchlands. Mokosza willing, she'd arrive in time.

No sound of hooves followed, and she drew to a

halt, looking over her shoulder, her heart racing. "Kaspian?"

He lowered his chin, his eyebrows knitted together over his blindfold. "Brygida, I'm sorry... I have to go to my father."

"Sorry?" Her eyes burned, and her throat constricted so tightly she could barely breathe. He was abandoning her, her mothers, *now*? When his own people were coming to kill them? There was no way she could placate the villagers herself; she'd have to fight them, and if some were women, she'd...

"My father is..." Kaspian shook his head.

His father had been dying for months.

"We'll join you," Nikodem said, his gaze locking with hers as he rode up to her side. His sister joined him, as did Stefan.

Brygida nodded her thanks to them and prayed they could sway the villagers. With a final disbelieving glance at Kaspian, she urged her horse to speed, as fast as it would go.

"Brygida!" Kaspian called out, but his mother's voice quickly intervened.

As Brygida's mount tore up the Rubin countryside in a frantic gallop, her stomach twisted, and hot tears streaked her face. She could understand it. His father might die today, after Mama had treated him and prolonged his life as best she could. He'd left his father alone all this time he'd searched for his mother, knowing his father could have died at any moment. He must've made his peace with that. And now that *her* mothers were in mortal danger from *his* people, he was sorry.

She could understand it. She could understand it, but she couldn't accept it.

No matter how she tried to calm herself, her heart pounded in her throat, and the black crescent on her hand burned.

Urszula, Nikodem, and Stefan followed her down the deer path to the cottage, where in the distance, its open door swung in the wind.

Another open doorway haunted her mind just then, and a burnt cottage.

Gasping, she jumped from the saddle, landing hard in the melting snow and scrambling to her feet. *Please,* she prayed. She didn't want to see a black hearth with no fire, a black table overturned, black dishes and black jars in pieces upon the black floor...

She stumbled through the doorway into her home, where the table she'd sat around with Mama and Mamusia had been overturned, broken pots and crushed herbs lying scattered.

"Brygida?" Paling, Mama stood in her old leather armor before the chest at the foot of her and Mamusia's bed, stringing a recurve bow. Her old recurve bow. She dashed toward Brygida, taking her in her arms. "Praise the Mother, you're safe."

Holding Mama close, she looked over her shoulder. "Where's Mamusia?"

Mama pulled away, her expression hard. "They came for her, but I don't know where they took her. I'm going to track them down."

The ghostly scream of a dying witch echoed in her mind, and the crescent mark burned. "I know where they took her," she whispered, and bolted from the cottage.

It would take every bit of power she could muster to save Mamusia from the Mouth of Weles. The vial wouldn't be enough. The ice had melted over the lake, and she plunged herself neck deep into the icy waters of Mroczne Lake.

Pangs of cold speared her body, but she wouldn't let *them* harm Mamusia as they had Anita. Shivering from the freezing temperature, she called upon the power of her foremothers, gathering the full strength of her power, cloaking herself in lake water.

As she stepped out of the lake, Urszula, Nikodem, and Stefan stared at her in shock. Even Mama's eyes were wide.

"Are you insane?" Urszula asked. "What are you—"

"It's better not to ask questions," Stefan interjected, with a reassuring nod to Brygida.

Summoning the wrath of the blood, she climbed into her horse's saddle and held out an arm for Mama, who took it and mounted up behind her. The horse danced beneath her before she dug her heels in and raced toward the Mouth of Weles.

With the Scythe of the Mother in hand, every thicket and branch made way for them, parting for the horses, and she inhaled the voices of the wood, their warnings, their encouragement, and urged her horse even faster.

We are with you, the voices whispered in unison from the scythe.

Screaming cut the wintry air, echoing from the cavern behind the willows. Mamusia's screaming.

Something broke inside her as she pulled the horse to an abrupt stop. With a leap from the saddle, she drew the water from the earth around her, calling its power to ready at her hands.

Ahead, a crowd gathered, and an arrow loosed from behind her, finding its target in a village woman's back.

"Leave her be!" Mama shouted, her command reverberating through the cavern.

The villagers held Mamusia bound in ropes above them, preparing to toss her into the gaping Mouth of Weles. She wriggled around, trying to free herself, the whites of her eyes showing as she locked gazes with her and Mama.

"Stop!" Stefan called out, rushing toward them. "Lady Rubin is back at the manor, and the demon that killed Paweł Kowal is slain!"

"Lies!" one of the women shouted back, a shining

horned-serpent pin on her dress. The mob brought Mamusia to the edge.

Mamusia's bound hands scrambled for their hair, their clothes, anything to keep her from being thrown into the abyss.

Brygida wept, balling her fists, the water at their call churning.

Mamusia's captors were all women.

If she harmed them, she'd lose the wrath of the blood. But if she didn't, she'd lose Mamusia.

Mama's bowstring twanged again, and an arrow embedded into the neck of one of the villagers.

A few scattered, but more remained.

She wouldn't let them. No matter the cost, she wouldn't let them. If this was the last time she could call upon the wrath of the blood, then she wouldn't leave a single one of the bloodthirsty humans standing.

"Brygida, no!" Mamusia called out around the strip of cloth stretched over her mouth.

Drawing as much water to her call as she could, Brygida forced it all in long, low spears stabbing toward the mob. Blades of ice spurted blood, cutting through feet, legs, thighs, and hips, and more as the injured humans fell to the ground in screams.

All of the ice melted instantly. And a small group of humans remained standing, holding Mamusia, their lives having been shielded by the deaths of the others before them.

She called upon the wrath, but nothing happened.

She eyed the Scythe of the Mother's blade, summoning the ice, but it didn't appear.

Mama's bow loosed arrow after arrow, but a din of voices rose up behind them.

Men carrying crude weapons, pitchforks and broken branches. Urszula and Nikodem leveled their swords at the flanking mob.

"We are not your enemies," Stefan said to them, drawing his own sword. "We don't have to do this!"

"Oh, I'm afraid we do." A many-ringed hand raised a blade. Dariusz.

"We'll handle them," Nikodem called back to her. "Do what you must!"

They rushed forward, scattering the group. Every-thing was chaos, but she turned back to Mamusia.

With no wrath of the blood to call upon.

With the voices of the Scythe of the Mother silent.

With nothing but her hands to fight for her. Even drenched in Mroczne lake water, she could do nothing as she watched the human women push Mamusia toward the Mouth of Weles, so ready to kill a witch who'd dedicated her life to protecting them. They dragged her at their side, shielding themselves from Mama's arrows as she was forced to lower her bow.

"Please, don't!" Mama called, her voice faltering. She extended a hand, but the humans ignored her. She ran toward the group, pulling them back, yanking their arms, trying to grasp for Mamusia, and Brygida ran after her, attempting to do the same to no avail.

Mokosza, please spare her. Perun, strike them with Your lightning, I beg You. Don't let Mamusia die.

At the rim, Mamusia screamed, the sound of it twisting her heart to pieces. The mark on Brygida's hand throbbed, the ache reaching to her fingertips as she closed her hand into a fist.

Weles, hear my prayer! Give me Your strength to stop them!

The mark pulsed again.

From the Mouth of the Weles, a darkness rose up from the depths. It slid out and across the cavern's floor. It seeped up the figures of the humans carrying Mamusia, pouring into their eyes, their noses, their mouths.

They screamed and fell to their knees.

Mama grasped Mamusia's arm and pulled her backward, hitting the ground together. "Liliana!" Mama cried, embracing Mamusia.

The darkness slithered past them and toward the men fighting Urszula, Nikodem, and Stefan.

It climbed the attacking humans' bodies, invaded their faces. Those it touched fell to the ground, black ooze draining from their eyes, noses, ears, and mouths.

Horrified humans gaped, turned, and ran, among them Dariusz. But none could escape its reach. The screaming rolled in waves that faded... faded... died.

After a few moments, silence reclaimed the forest.

And the bodies of her enemies lay at her feet. What lingering traces of the darkness remained now meandered toward her, and she closed her eyes, ready to meet the same fate as the dead humans.

She waited... and waited... and waited.

But that fate never came.

As she opened her eyes, the final tendrils of darkness absorbed into her crescent mark.

Shaking, she looked to her mothers, who held out their arms to her. She ran to them, and the three of them held on to one another. For a long while, they just held each other, crying quiet tears of relief.

Mamusia grabbed Brygida's hand, turning it over and inspecting it, and frowned sadly. And then she looked around at the bodies and to Stefan, Urszula, and Nikodem, who stood by, staring at the fallen in horror.

Something dark and disturbing had risen from her in those moments when she'd prayed to Weles, something from her mark.

"You've killed women," Mamusia stammered, tears rolling down her cheeks. "You can't stay here any longer, Brygida."

And the world shattered.

CHAPTER 25

Kaspian sat at the edge of the bed. His parents'
room was as stifling hot as it had been before,
and the stench of herbs just as overpowering.
Mama knelt at the bedside, Tata's hand in hers.

His vision was returning, slowly. He could make out
blurred shapes and more color, but he didn't need to
see Tata to know this really was the end. Each breath
was a wheeze, and he could not even raise his hand
from the blanket.

"Sabina?" Tata rasped, and then coughed.

"I'm here, don't worry. I'm here now." She brushed
the hair from his eyes.

He took a rattling breath. "I"—he gasped—"should
have done"—another gasp—"better by you."

"Hush, don't." Mama leaned in, stroking Tata's face
gently.

"Kaspian?" Tata's unfocused gaze looked around the room.

Kaspian moved in closer, so Tata wouldn't have to strain further. "I'm here, Tata." The emotion was thick in his throat.

Losing Roksana had been hard enough, and losing Tata as well felt cruel, with everything left unresolved. There was no more time to go back, to recapture the time they'd lost to bitter words and misunderstandings. Knowing death had been coming hadn't made it any easier to process.

He stroked Tata's hand with his thumb. These strong hands had once picked him up to ride on his shoulders, had swung him around to his delightful squeals.

"Be... a good... lord." Each word was followed by a rattling gasp, as if Tata couldn't get enough air.

"I will, Tata. I promise." Although he'd tried to fight them back, the tears leaked from his eyes.

Thank Perun he'd made it back before it was too late. He'd let his anger and bitterness blind him, but for Tata's sake and his own, he was determined to do right, to listen to Mama's wisdom, and to lead Rubin's people to prosperity.

Tata closed his eyes, and his breathing slowed. Mama put her arm around him. As they held one another close, through the pain and grief, the minutes turned to hours as they kept vigil at Tata's bedside. And then without warning and without fanfare, Tata slipped away.

In the blink of an eye, he was gone.

Grief struck him like a blow to the gut. Tata's suffering was over, but it didn't lessen the pain of his loss. He'd thought he'd known the pain of grief after losing Roksana, but it wasn't finite, didn't make losing his father any easier. His heart bled from a fresh wound, and Tata's dying wish weighed heavily upon it.

He'd be a good lord. He would.

⊗※⊗

BRYGIDA SAT AT THE TABLE TOGETHER WITH HER mothers, grasping one another's hands. Mamusia brushed her thumb over Brygida's black scar. She'd passed Weles's test, gained his favor by defeating the bies, but by harming women, she'd become disfavored of Mokosza. Fallen.

"I'm sorry to both of you. If I had listened in the first place, none of this would ever have happened," she said as she squeezed both her mothers' hands. It had been blind foolishness to think her witchlands and this cottage had been a cage, that her mothers had been her jailers. This was home, and now it was lost to her.

"You'll have to find a way to repent," Mamusia whispered, her violet eyes welling with tears as she stroked her cheek with a loving hand. "Mokosza is gracious, and I pray there will be a time when you can return to us."

The very thought of leaving made her sick. But it had been her choice. She'd chosen Mamusia's life over that of the humans, and now she had to pay the price.

Tears streamed down her face. Even knowing what she must do, why did it hurt so deeply?

Mamusia stood and came around to wrap Brygida in her embrace, and then Mama joined her. She wanted to stay here in the comfort and safety of their arms, to never let go. But her place here was gone, by her own hand.

Outside, Urszula and Nikodem awaited.

She buried her face in Mama's shoulder, inhaling the comforting and familiar amber scent for the last time. "I will find a way to atone, I promise." She clung to Mamusia's back as she rubbed there gently.

"And we will be here waiting for you, always," Mamusia said.

Now. Now was the time to leave before she became a heap of tears on the floor. If she didn't go by dusk, Mokosza would withdraw her protection from Rubin, and she wouldn't stay here long enough to force Mamusia into a difficult position.

As she pulled away, Mama grabbed Brygida's shoulder and squeezed. "I'm proud of you, Brygida. Without me realizing it, you've grown from a child to a woman. Trust your heart, and be safe."

Brygida nodded, wiped the tears from her eyes, and headed for the door. Mama and Mamusia handed her a pack of supplies and her cloak.

Urszula and Nikodem were saddled and waiting. "Ready?"

"There's one last thing I need to do." Whatever had happened, she couldn't leave Rubin without saying goodbye to Kaspian.

They nodded and headed through the forest, back down the deer path toward the Perun-struck oak. As she traveled, the chill creeped into her bones, and when she inhaled, the voices of the wood were silent. The forest loomed over her as it never had, making her feel unwelcome and unwanted.

The bies was gone, but the forest was not appeased. She'd spilled blood here, and it would not rest until she was far away. And hopefully in time, she could win back Mokosza's favor.

Branches tangled together, making the forest a labyrinth of knotted pathways, and all around her, she felt eyes watching.

At the Perun-struck oak, at the border between worlds, she stopped, while Urszula and Nikodem forged ahead to the crossroads, where they'd await her.

Beneath the dead boughs, a lone figure already stood, camouflaged against the trunk. Somehow, Kaspian was waiting for her, holding in his arms her headdress and her bear fur.

It had only been a little over a week, but Kolęda seemed a lifetime ago. Without her calling to him, he turned to greet her with a half-smile. He opened his arms, welcoming her into an embrace it hurt to see.

She should have rejected him, but her feet didn't listen, taking her to him, to the circle of his arms, hands clutching at the back of his shirt. She breathed him in, the scent of paints long faded from his skin, but he didn't smell of spirits either.

More than anything she wanted to enshrine this moment with him, to cling onto it and never let go. But what had passed between them when they'd returned to Czarnobrzeg was like the bies's crack in her mind, widening and widening no matter how hard she tried to keep both worlds together. In trying to bridge them, she'd nearly lost him, her mothers, and herself.

If there was a way forward for them, it didn't look anything like what they'd traveled so far, and they still needed to find a bridge for the hairline crack between them. But she had to answer to her goddess. And she had to leave to do so.

After a few minutes, she pulled back. "I... I can't. I need to tell you something."

"I have something to tell you as well." A deep sadness shadowed his gaze. Perhaps Stefan had already told him. "You first."

She inhaled deeply. "I'm leaving, and I don't know when I'll be able to return, if ever."

The tightening lines of his face were a stab to her gut. "But why?"

That night in the barn, he'd talked about running away together. It seemed so distant now.

"I've betrayed everything I've ever known. And I have to make amends."

There was a long pause.

"I see." His response was cold, and so unlike him. "You're leaving and might never return." His eyebrow twitched, his breath ragged for a moment before he bobbed his head. "Then this is where you tell me goodbye?"

The tears she had yet to shed threatened to burst from her, but it would only make leaving harder. "By Her thread, Kaspian."

Pressing his lips firmly together, he turned.

"Wait," she said, taking a couple steps toward him. "What was it you wanted to tell me?"

"My father died today," he said, barely glancing backward. "Goodbye, Brygida." And with those final parting words, he walked away.

She reached out for him, half-hoping he would turn around, but he never did. If she chased after him now, she would take him in her arms, whisper words of comfort, and never let him go, never leave, and the sun was already beginning to set.

Tears streamed down her face as she watched him go, and once he'd disappeared from sight, she headed for the crossroads.

As she joined Urszula and Nikodem, a raven landed on the branch overhead, cawing. Had Mokosza not completely abandoned her after all? "Don't tease me, messenger," she whispered.

It flew along the road to Granat, and with her two companions, she followed.

CHAPTER 26

The winter winds lingered longer than they had in years past. Or was it just that the days seemed longer? Grief had a funny way of distorting time. Kaspian had thrown himself into his work, preparing for the spring planting, absorbing all he could about lordship from Mama, and yet it was never enough to distract him. Working in Tata's study, there were a hundred different reminders of him. His books, the phantom scent of him that clung to the tapestry and the chair. At any moment, he expected Tata to walk in through that door and scold him for daring to sit in his place.

But this was who he was now. Lord of Rubin.

He had accepted his fate. The duty he had run from had nearly cost him Mama. There was no turning back now.

Outside the window, the clouds rolled away and shafts of sunlight illuminated the winter woods. Brygida's home. Just thinking of her was like a dagger to his heart. And although many times he'd thought of expressing his feelings by painting, he couldn't bring himself to lift a brush. Or to leave this room, for that matter.

The time he'd spent with Brygida had been as ephemeral as a snowflake, a shining stolen moment in time that would melt away come spring. Even if he had the choice, he could never hold onto her. He could see that now. No matter how hard he'd tried, how hard they'd tried, their worlds were just too different, and as the spring took the snows, so too their relationship had to come to an end.

A lord's duty was to his people, and a witch's duty was to her witchlands. As much as he loved her, there was no way forward that he could see yet.

"Kaspian, are you paying attention?"

He jerked his head up. Mama stood over his desk, arms crossed over her chest.

"Mm." He picked up the paper on his desk, pretending to scan it, but all the words blurred together. "Yes, lambs, crops, important things," he teased with a mockingly serious nod.

"Kaspian, this isn't a game. If we don't plant enough, come spring the entire region will starve."

"I am well aware." He stood up, putting aside the papers he could not focus on if he tried. "It will all work out, because you're here to guide me."

She gave him a playful slap. "Don't try and flatter your way out of this one."

Try as he might, he couldn't push Brygida out of his mind. He'd have to try harder. "Why don't we go for a walk, like we used to when I was younger?"

She shook her head. "There's really so much to do."

He hooked his arm through hers. "Just a short one. Isn't this study too stuffy? I think it is."

She laughed. "Is this some sort of trick so you can go off and see that witch?"

He tensed. It had been days since anyone had even said a whisper about Brygida, and even Stefan had held back from teasing for once.

She'd left him, perhaps for good, she'd said. He needed to force himself to move on. "I've been thinking... Perhaps you could find me a suitable bride?" Forcing out the words hurt. He didn't want it, couldn't even fathom it, but how else could he move on?

"Are you sure?" Mama arched an eyebrow.

He nodded. "Let's say that I am."

She rested her hand over his. "Maybe we should go for that walk after all."

Just then, there was a knock at the door.

"Come in," Mama called.

The serving woman entered, her head bowed. The sunlight from the window glinted off something that she wore on her apron.

"It's lunch time, my lady, my lord," she murmured.

"We'll take it later, thank you. My son and I are going for a walk."

The serving woman bobbed her head and turned to leave, and as she did, Kaspian caught sight of the pin.

The horned snake. The symbol of the Cult of Weles.

They were here, in the village.

THE COTTAGE CAME INTO VIEW JUST AS BRYGIDA'S EYES started to grow heavy. The raven was exceedingly patient with them, leading them through tangled forests and through unfamiliar landscapes. And now it landed on the roof of the burnt cottage, squawking loudly.

"Are you sure this is where you want to be?" Urszula asked, head canted.

"Perhaps you should stay at the manor," Nikodem said, and cleared his throat. "This place is unsettling."

She had never lived outside of a forest, and she doubted she'd feel comfortable for long on Lord Granat's hospitality. Anita's cottage in the woods had called to her. And the raven had led her here.

This was where she belonged.

Brygida slid out of the saddle and approached the cottage. It would take some work and effort, but she could get it cleaned up and livable.

"No, this is where I'll stay."

Urszula climbed down from the saddle.

"Well, if you're going to be stubborn, let's at least chop you some firewood so you don't freeze to death." She went into a nearby shed, which seemed to have been spared the worst of the fire.

Nikodem went inside and surveyed the interior. "I could help with this, if you don't mind an intruder here from time to time over the next few weeks."

She smiled faintly. "How about a guest?"

A muscle twitched in his jaw as he bobbed his head with amusement.

Between the three of them, they were able to clear away the snow that had propped the door open, removed the worst of the burnt furniture's remains, and scavenged together a bed. With Urszula's efforts, there was now enough firewood to last her for a few days.

The sun was starting to set by the time they were done.

"We'll be back tomorrow with supplies and to check on you," Nikodem said in parting.

"Thank you." She watched them go, and once they disappeared into the trees, she found her way back inside.

Alone in the empty hut, without even a table and

chairs, the weight of her isolation was nearly crushing. Taking a steady breath, she went into her pack and pulled out Anita's grimoire.

Anita had no successor, this forest was waking, and Mokosza had cast her out. What better place could there be for her to start a new life, to find some way to make recompense for her sins?

She knelt on the floor, her knee creaking over the loose floorboard. She picked it up, then reached for the Scythe of the Mother below.

END OF BOOK TWO

Thanks for reading *Fate of the Demon*! If you enjoyed the adventure, please consider leaving a review. The review rating determines which series we prioritize, so if you want more books in this series soon, review this one!

Ready for the next installment in the Witch of the Lake series? The next book is called *Fall of the Reaper*, available now.

Should it wake, its nightmares will consume the world...

After her life nearly fell apart, Brygida finally knows her place: away from the village, healing the slumbering wood to keep the nightmares at bay. Her grimoire warns that the wood may never be allowed to wake, and she claims that duty for her own. Her mind does turn to the new lord of Rubin, but wishing for more almost lost her everything, and she's not about to lose her witchlands to its nightmares caused by the villagers. That is, until the dreaded cult arrives...

Kaspian has never wanted the rulership, but when his father passes away, he has no choice but to ascend to lord. With tensions high between the village and the witches, trust lacking between him and his subjects, and a heavy heart turned toward the wood, Kaspian can't help but wish for someone to take it all away... And then a familiar face from his past comes to grant it.

With a tide of blood and demons in its wake, the cult arrives to cleanse the so-called stain of witchcraft upon Rubin, and it won't stop until Brygida and her mothers are dead. But with demons closing in and the fitfully slumbering wood ready to wake, the cult's spark of violence could destroy not only the region of Rubin, but everything. Desperate for allies, betrayed by blood, and alienated from one another, can Brygida and Kaspian stem the dark tide of the cult together, or will they, their people, their lands, and everything drown in the mortal inevitability of blood, demons, and a waking wood with an insatiable hunger...?

Find out what happens when the slumbering wood wakes in FALL OF THE REAPER, the thrilling third book in this romantic dark fantasy series inspired by Slavic mythology and folklore, sure to please fans of

Juliet Marillier's Blackthorn & Grim series and Naomi Novik's Uprooted.

Read *Fall of the Reaper* to unearth the secrets of this beautifully haunting adventure today!

PRONUNCIATION GUIDE

- Agata Duma: "ah-GAH-tah DOO-mah"
- Albert Malicki: "AHL-behrt Mah-LEETS-kee"
- Andrzej: "ON-dzhey"
- bies: "BYESS"
- błędnica: "bwend-NEETS-ah"
- Bogdan: "BOHG-dahn"
- Brygida Mrok: "brih-GHEE-dah Mrohk"
- chorobnik: "hoh-ROBE-neek"
- Czarnobrzeg: "char-NOH-bzheg"
- Dariusz Baran: "DAHR-yoosh BAH-rahn"
- Demon: "DEH-mon"
- Dażbóg: "DAHZH-boog"
- Dorota Duma: "doh-ROH-tah DOO-mah"
- drak: "DRAHK"
- Dziewanna: "djeh-VAHN-nah"

- Ewa Mrok: "EH-vah Mrohk"
- Gerard: "GHEH-rahrd"
- gęśla: "GHEWSCH-lah"
- Granat: "GRAH-not"
- Halina: "hah-LEE-nah"
- Henryk Wolski: "HEN-rihk VOHL-skee"
- Iga Mrok: "EE-gah Mrohk"
- Iskra: "EES-krah"
- Julian Zając: "YOOL-yan ZAH-yohntz"
- Kaspian Wolski: "KAHS-pyahn VOHL-skee"
- Kolęda: "kohl-EN-dah"
- lasowik: "lah-SOH-veek"; [pl. lasowiki: "lah-soh-VEE-kee"]
- lejiń: "LEH-yeen"; [pl. lejinie: "leh-YEE-nyeh"]
- leśna nimfa: "LESH-nah NEEM-fah"
- leszy: "LEH-shih" [pl. lesze: "LEH-sheh"]
- Liliana Mrok: "leel-YAH-nah Mrohk"
- Łukasz Wolski: "WOO-kash VOHL-skee"
- maleńka: "mah-LEN-kah"
- mamon: "mah-MOHN"
- Mamusia: "mah-MOO-shah"
- Mokosza: "Moh-KOH-shah"
- Mroczne: "MROCH-neh"
- Nikodem: "nee-KOH-dem"
- Nina Baran: "NEE-nah BAH-rahn"
- Nizina: "nee-ZEE-nah"

- Oskar Grobowski: "OHS-kahr groh-BOHF-skee"
- Perun: "PEH-roon"
- polewik: "poh-LEH-veek" [pl. polewiki: "Poh-leh-VEE-kee"]
- Rafał: "RAH-fahw"
- Roksana Malicka: "rok-SAH-nah mah-LEETS-kah"
- Rubin: "ROO-been"
- rusałka: "roo-SOW-kah" [pl. rusałki: "roo-SOW-kee"]
- Sabina Wolska: "sah-BEE-nah VOHL-skah"
- Skawa: "SKAH-vah"
- Stefan Bania: "STEH-fahn BAH-nyah"
- Stryjek: "STRIH-yek"
- Swaróg: "SFAH-roog"
- Tarnowice: "rar-noh-VEE-tzeh"
- Tata: "TAH-tah"
- Teresa Malicka: "teh-REH-sah mah-LEETS-kah"
- Urszula: "ur-SHOO-lah"
- Weles: "VEL-es"
- Wilk: "VEELK"
- wilkołak: "veel-KOH-wok"
- Zofia Baran: "ZOHF-yah BAH-rahn"

AUTHORS' NOTE

As always, this book wouldn't have been possible without the help of a great many people. We are so grateful for the feedback from authors like J.M. Butler and Katherine Bennet, who helped us work out the bumps in the manuscript before it landed in your hands.

We're also thankful for the proofreading efforts of Anthony S. Holabird and Lea Vickery, who caught our errors so they wouldn't disrupt your reading! (Any possible leftover typos are *our* mistakes, and not theirs.) K.D. Ritchie from Storywrappers also lent her considerable talents to provide us with the cover of our dreams!

And you, our readers: we owe you everything. Without you, this story (and our careers) wouldn't exist. Thank you so much for supporting us and these yarns of fantastical madness we get to weave.

ABOUT MIRANDA HONFLEUR

Miranda Honfleur is a born-and-raised Chicagoan living in Indianapolis. She grew up on fantasy and science fiction novels, spending nearly as much time in Valdemar, Pern, Tortall, Narnia, and Middle Earth as in reality.

In another life, her J.D. and M.B.A. were meant to serve a career in law, but now she gets to live her dream job: writing speculative fiction starring fierce heroines and daring heroes who make difficult choices along their adventures and intrigues, all with a generous (over)dose of romance.

When she's not snarking, writing, or reading her Kindle, she hangs out and watches Netflix with her English-teacher husband and plays board games with her friends.

Reach her at:
www.mirandahonfleur.com
miri@mirandahonfleur.com
https://www.patreon.com/honfleur

f facebook.com/mirandahonfleur

twitter.com/MirandaHonfleur

a amazon.com/author/mirandahonfleur

BB bookbub.com/authors/miranda-honfleur

g goodreads.com/mirandahonfleur

instagram.com/mirandahonfleur

ABOUT NICOLETTE ANDREWS

Nicolette Andrews is a native San Diegan with a passion for the world of make-believe. From a young age, Nicolette was telling stories, whether it was writing plays for her friends to act out or making a series of children's books that her mother still likes drag out to embarrass her in front of company.

She still lives in her imagination, but in reality she resides in San Diego with her husband, children and a couple cats. She loves reading, attempting arts and crafts, and cooking.

You can visit her at her website:
www.fantasyauthornicoletteandrews.com
or at these places:

facebook.com/nicandfantasy
twitter.com/nicandfantasy
instagram.com/nicolette_andrews
bookbub.com/authors/nicolette-andrews
pinterest.com/Nicandfantasy
amazon.com/author/nicoletteandrews

BIBLIOGRAPHY

We couldn't have written this book without the wonderful resources, both in Polish and in English, on various historical and mythological aspects that helped us immensely.

Bobrowski, Jakub, Mateusz Wrona, and Błażej Ostoja-Lniski. *Czarty, Biesy, Zjawy: Opowieści z Pańskiego Stołu.* N.p.: Bosz, 2019. Print.

Bobrowski, Jakub, Mateusz Wrona, and Magdalena Boffito. *Mitologia Słowiańska.* N.p.: Wydawnictwo Bosz Szymanik i Wspólnicy, 2018. Print.

Cunningham, Scott. *Cunningham's Encyclopedia of Magical Herbs.* St. Paul, MN: Llewellyn Publications, 2016. Print.

Debuigne, Gérard, François Couplan, Pierre Vignes, Délia Vignes, and Katarzyna Cedro. *Wielki Zielnik Roślin Leczniczych*. Kielce: Wydawnictwo Jedność, 2019. Print.

Dębek, Bogusław Andrzej. *Początki Ludów: Europejczycy, Słowianie*. N.p.: Bellona, 2019. Print.

Gieysztor, Aleksander, Karol Modzelewski, Leszek Paweł Słupecki, and Aneta Pieniądz. *Mitologia Słowian*. N.p.: Wydawnictwa Uniwersytetu Warszawskiego, 2018. Print.

Kajkowski, Kamil. *Mity, Kult i Rytuał: O Duchowości Nadbałtyckich Słowian*. N.p.: Triglav, 2017. Print.

Knab, Sophie Hodorowicz. *Polish Customs, Traditions and Folklore*. New York: Hippocrene, 2017. Print.

Lehner, Ernst. *Folklore and Symbolism of Flowers, Plants and Trees*. Martino Fine, 2012. Print.

Moszyński, Kazimierz, and Jadwiga Klimaszewska. *Kultura Ludowa Słowian*. N.p.: Grafika Usługi Wydawnicze Iwona Knechta, 2010. Print.

Moszyński, Kazimierz, and Jadwiga Klimaszewska. *Kultura Ludowa Słowian*. N.p.: Grafika Usługi Wydawnicze Iwona Knechta, 2010. Print.

Moszyński, Kazimierz, Jadwiga Klimaszewska, and Maria Bytnar-Suboczowa. *Kultura Ludowa Słowian*. N.p.: Grafika Usługi Wydawnicze Iwona Knechta, 2010. Print.

Pankalla, Andrzej, and Konrad Kazimierz Kośnik. *Indygeniczna Psychologia Słowian: Wprowadzenie Do Realnej Nauki o Duszy*. N.p.: TAiWPN UNIVERSITAS, 2018. Print.

Pobiegły, Elżbieta, and Ewa Rossal. *Stroje Krakowskie: Historie i Mity: Praca Zbiorowa*. Krakow: Muzeum Etnograficzne Im. Seweryna Udzieli, 2017. Print.

Strzelczyk, Jerzy. *Bohaterowie Słowian Połabskich*. N.p.: Wydawnictwo Poznańskie, 2017. Print.

Szczepanik, Paweł. *Słowiańskie Zaświaty: Wierzenia, Wizje i Mity*. Szczecin: Triglav, 2018. Print.

Szrejter, Artur. *Pod Pogańskim Sztandarem: Dzieje Tysiąca Wojen Słowian Połabskich Od VII Do XII Wieku*. Warszawa: Instytut Wydawniczy Erica, 2016. Print.

Vargas, Witold, and Paweł Zych. *Magiczne Zawody: Kowal, Czarodziej, Alchemik*. N.p.: Bosz, 2018. Print.

Zielina, Jakub. *Wierzenia Prasłowian*. Kraków: Wydawnictwo Petrus, 2014. Print.

CPSIA information can be obtained
at www.ICGtesting.com
Printed in the USA
LVHW030838271220
675096LV00005B/768

9 781949 932164

Zych, Paweł, and Witold Vargas. *Bestiariusz Słowiański*.
N.p.: Bosz, 2018. Print.